Ox-Tales
AIR

*Original stories from
remarkable writers*

P

Ox-Tales are published in support of

😕 Oxfam

First published in Great Britain in 2009 by *Green*Profile, an imprint of
Profile Books Ltd, 3A Exmouth House, Pine Street, London EC1R 0JH

Printed in the UK by CPI Bookmarque, Croydon, CR0 4TD
Typeset in Iowan to a design by Sue Lamble

1 3 5 7 9 10 8 6 4 2

A CIP catalogue record for this book is
available from the British Library
ISBN: 978 1 84668 261 2

Ox-Tales: Air

OX-TALES: AIR is one of four original collections, featuring stories by leading British- and Irish-based writers. Each of the writers has contributed their story for free in order to raise money and awareness for Oxfam. The FOUR ELEMENTS provide a loose framework for the stories and highlight key areas of Oxfam's work: water projects (WATER), aid for conflict areas (FIRE), agricultural development (EARTH), and action on climate change (AIR). An afterword, at the end of each book, explains how Oxfam makes a difference. And in buying this book, you'll be a part of that process, too.

Compiling these books, we asked authors for new stories; or, from novelists who don't do short stories, work in progress from their next book. The response was thirty-eight original pieces of fiction, which are spread across the four books and framed by a cycle of element poems by Vikram Seth. We think they're extraordinary, but be your own judge. And if you like what you read here, please buy all four OX-TALES books – and help Oxfam work towards an end to poverty worldwide.

Mark Ellingham (Profile) & Peter Florence (Hay Festival)
Editors, OX-TALES

Acknowledgments

The Ox-Tales books were developed at Profile Books by Mark Ellingham in association with Peter Florence and Hay Festival. Thanks from us both to the authors who contributed stories – and time – to creating these four collections in support of Oxfam. And thanks, too, to their publishers and agents who, without exception, offered generous support to this project.

At Oxfam, Tom Childs has guided the project alongside Suzy Smith, Charlie Hayes, Annie Lewis, Fee Gilfeather, Annemarie Papatheofilou and Matt Kurton.

At Profile, Peter Dyer, Penny Daniel, Niamh Murray, Duncan Clark, Claire Beaumont, Simon Shelmerdine, Ruth Killick, Rebecca Gray, Kate Griffin and Andrew Franklin have been instrumental. Thanks also to Nikky Twyman and Caroline Pretty for proofreading, and to Jonathan Gray for his cover illustrations.

Contents

VIKRAM SETH (born Calcutta, India, 1952) is the author of the novels *The Golden Gate* (1986), *A Suitable Boy* (1993) and *An Equal Music* (1999), and of books of poetry, travel, fable and memoir.

'Air' is part of a sequence of poems, *Seven Elements*, incorporating the elements in the European, Indian and Chinese traditions (earth, air, fire, water, wood, metal and space). Set to music by the composer Alec Roth, *Seven Elements* will be performed in summer 2009 at the Salisbury, Chelsea and Lichfield festivals.

Air

Air from your lips makes me vibrate,
Who am a tube of air,
And I make ripples where
Singing, singing,
I speak of joy and soothe the erratic pulse of hate.

Air from the sky slips past my arms
And buoys my tube of air
And thrusts me forward where
Winging, winging,
I soar above all earthly frenzies and alarms.

I am the stuff of death and birth,
Of wreck and of repair,
The unseen skin of air –
Clinging, clinging
To wrap and save for life the injured crust of earth.

Vikram Seth

Still Life

ALEXANDER McCALL SMITH (born Zimbabwe, 1948) is the author of over sixty books on a wide array of subjects. For many years he was Professor of Medical Law at the University of Edinburgh and served on national and international bioethics bodies. He is best known as the creator of *The No. 1 Ladies' Detective Agency* series, set in Botswana. He plays the bassoon in The Really Terrible Orchestra.

1

IN SOME PARTS of the Scottish Highlands there are glens that are accessible only by sea. No roads go to these places, only sheep tracks, or paths that disappear after heavy rains or the run-off from winter snows. Sea lochs, though, are always there, often protected from the Atlantic as it sweeps round the coast of Scotland, and a small boat from a harbour further down the coast may slip through these waters and make land safely.

Life in such places was not always lonely. Even after the Highland clearances had destroyed many of the villages that clung to the hillsides, there were still small settlements of people who lived by crofting. Along the shores of this particular sea loch, there were several families who survived until the 1950s by fishing and the raising of a few sheep and cattle. Here and there a greater level of prosperity resulted when a promising boy had been sent off to Glasgow or Edinburgh to study medicine or engineering. Money would be sent back home to ease the plight of those who had stayed behind. Shoes would be bought.

2

But now, along the shores of this loch, even the few crofts that sustained such families had fallen into disrepair. Roofs had fallen in and the exposed timbers had rotted in the damp sea air; the blocks of rough-hewn grey stone that made up the walls had tumbled as their lime pointing flaked and fell out of its bedding – in this way a house would become a shell and then not much more than a cairn. Eventually only irregular ridges in the soil would remain, the footprint of what was once a house; such mounds can be seen throughout the west of Scotland, where the land is a palimpsest on which the history of a people is written. It is natural to imagine that this history is a sorrowful one, but only parts of it were. People who have suffered often illuminate their lives with song and with joy. So the echoes to be heard in this place are not uniformly ones of sorrow.

3

At the head of this loch, at a place where a small river made its way into the sea, a large house had been built. It was a cross between a shooting lodge and the house of a prosperous farmer, and around it a Highland estate had been created for a Glasgow industrialist, a ship-builder. He had deliberately picked somewhere that would be inaccessible except by sea; a remote place far from the industrial sprawl, the din, the clanging of rivets on which his fortune was based. Great wealth sometimes seeks simplicity, curiously mirroring the lives of those whose labours produce the wealth in the first place. This man lived frugally and by and large treated his employees on the estate generously, if paternalistically. He was by no means insensitive to the economic plight of others; he had added his voice to the protests that had led to the freeing of John Maclean, the red Clydesider, who he felt had a point, even if that point meant that people like him would cease to exist as a class.

4

When he died, he had a clear conscience.

5

The house passed into the hands of the ship-builder's daughter, a woman who had been married, briefly, to an Edinburgh advocate. The advocate was faithless and conducted a prolonged affair with the wife of a banker. The banker hated the advocate and wished him dead. They had the misfortune of being members of the same golf club, and on a couple of occasions met on the greens. The banker did his best to conceal with shame, his anger, but was sick in the bunker after his rival had passed by. No words were exchanged beyond the curtest of greetings that civility and the unwritten rules of the club required. Eventually the advocate's wife left him, taking her daughter with her. That was in 1970. In 1995, the house became the property of this daughter, then aged thirty-five. Ten years later, this woman, who had been married to a painter, found herself alone. The painter could not take the isolation; nor did he like the north, where he said the air was too attenuated for him.

'I still love you,' he said to his wife. 'I really do. But I was not meant to live in a place like this. I belong further south. That's all there is to it. I can't stay here. Look at my painting. It's withering. The air is wrong – it's just wrong.'

She looked at the air, as he urged her to do. She saw only blue; the air that came in off the Atlantic, just beyond the mouth of the sea loch, the air that carried on its breath the tang of sea-weed and the exhalations of the ocean; the air that she had lived with for so long and that sustained her, and this place she loved so much. When she went to a city – which was very infrequently – she felt that she was on the verge of suffocation, for the very air in such places was sixth-hand, it seemed.

'I don't know what you're talking about,' she said. But then, almost immediately, she added: 'I suppose I do. You're a Mediterranean type at heart. You want that particular light. All right. You want that. I don't.'

He looked at her, as one might look at somebody whom one fears one has mortally wounded. 'You're not going to forgive me, are you?'

She smiled. 'Of course I shall forgive you. What do you take me for? We're adults. We belong in different places, that's all. Go to Montpelier. Go wherever. We can remain friends.'

'Separated by air.'

'Yes. Separated only by air.'

6

Other people lived there. She was alone in the house, but there was a factor's house – built in a good position near the water's edge – and two other small houses, one for the farm hand and one for the ghillie. The river near the house provided some salmon fishing and people came for grouse and stag shooting each season. That is what sustained the economy of the estate. It made no profit at all, but it paid its way through the progression of wealthy visitors who paid to trudge their way up into the hills above the sea loch and find sport there. She did not like shooting, and would kill nothing, but what alternative did she have if she was to keep the place afloat? The livelihood of more than one family was at stake here. The ghillie, alone, had five children, all of whom lived with their mother during the week, in the small harbour town round the point. If there were no visitors to pay his wages, they would have to leave the land. So there was no room for sentiment when she saw the poor dead stags hanging on the meat-hook. She had to avert her eyes, as we do all the time, about so many things.

7

One summer an Italian came to shoot stags. He had been sent, as they all were, by the sporting agency in Edinburgh. 'This chap's got some sort of sea-plane,' the agent said. 'He's insisting on flying up from Glasgow in it. We tried to put him off. We told him that the loch can get a bit choppy if the wind's in a certain quarter. He'd have none of it.'

'He's a dead man,' said the factor. 'The loch can look quiet enough and then suddenly a swell sneaks in and his wee plane will be on its back. I'm not going in to fish him out.'

'He must know what he's doing,' she said. 'He's probably an experienced pilot.'

The factor was not convinced. 'We'll see,' he said. 'This isn't Loch Como.'

'Lake Como.'

'Aye, that's what I said.'

The factor was a taciturn man, who tended to take a cautious view of things. He was not a real factor, of course, as the estate was far too small. A real factor dealt with tenants and rent and tradesmen fixing things – there was nothing like that up there: no rents, and if anything needed fixing then it would have to be fixed by the factor himself or by the farm hand, who was quite a craftsman. He made cromachs, with crooks made out of the horns of blackface rams. He sold these to a shop in Fort William, where there was a ready market for them in a shop that sold tartan rugs and recordings of sentimental Scottish crooners.

The factor did not have to have many dealings with the visitors. He rather resented them. The person who looked after them was the ghillie, who was also the keeper. He knew the hills intimately and could spot deer at a great distance. He knew the numbers of each herd down to the last deer and seemed to have an uncanny knack for knowing where they were headed. He drank, however, and always carried a full hip-flask of whisky with him when he was on the hill.

The Italians understood this, and smiled; American guests tended to be disapproving.

'It's our culture here,' the ghillie explained when he detected disapproval. 'In Scotland we drink.'

'Maybe,' a guest once said. 'But handling firearms does not go with alcohol. I'm not criticising you personally, you know; it's just a general observation.'

8

The Italian telephoned from Glasgow to say that he would be arriving later that afternoon. He spoke good English, and she had no difficulty understanding him.

'The weather is clear at the moment,' she said, looking out of the window. 'I don't think there will be much wind today.'

'I am told you have a mooring,' said the Italian. 'I'd like to tie my plane to that. I have an inflatable dinghy that I can come in on.'

'We can fetch you,' she said. 'The ghillie will come out.'

He did not understand the word 'ghillie', and she explained it to him. 'It is a very beautiful word, like Scotland itself. Very beautiful.'

'Italian is such a beautiful language too,' she said.

'But we have nothing that means ghillie,' he replied.

She put down the telephone and went to stand outside, on the lawn. She looked down the loch; the water was calm, like a blue mirror. If it was like that in the afternoon, then his little sea-plane would have no difficulty. She imagined it bobbing gently on the surface of the water, tied to the mooring, and the Italian rowing himself in his inflatable boat, waving to her, perhaps.

She looked up the letter from the agent to remind herself of his name. He was called Carlo, and she imagined that he would look a bit like Charles Edward Stuart, but with a slightly stronger face.

9

He arrived shortly after four. The sky was still clear, quite cloudless, and they had no trouble making out his small green sea-plane as it dropped down towards the loch.

'He's coming in far too fast,' said the factor. 'My God! Look at that. He's going to smack into the water. Break up.'

But the plane stopped its drop and levelled out. Then, quite elegantly, it settled itself on the surface of the water, casting a small cloud of white spray behind it. The engine note was like that of a buzz saw, high-pitched and insistent; after a few moments it stopped and they saw the individual blades of the propeller appear from their white whirring circle.

'He's made it,' said the factor. There was disappointment in his voice.

'You sound as if you wanted him to crash,' she said. 'You really are transparent, Jimmy. I can read you, you know.'

He was emphatic in his denial. 'I would never want anybody to crash.'

'Wouldn't you?'

He looked injured. 'Of course not.'

'I suppose you wouldn't.'

10

Carlo said that evening over pre-dinner drinks, 'I loved flying in today. That view as you arrive is wonderful. Just the few houses and the mountains behind them. The sea. I saw an eagle below me.'

'We are very proud of this place,' she said. 'It belonged to my grandfather. He built ships in Glasgow – or rather he had other people build them.'

'My great-grandfather had other people pick olives,' Carlo said. 'And then he had other people screw nuts and bolts together. That is how I have that plane. The efforts of others.'

'Like everything,' she said.

'It is a small plane,' he said. 'There are only two seats. Perhaps you will come for a ride in it.'

The factor, who was standing with his back to the fire, asked, 'Me?'

Carlo smiled. 'You too. Of course. But first I was offering to take Mrs … Mrs …'

'Jean.'

'To take Jean here. I think you would like it. If we take off towards the open sea, we can get over that hill down there – easily. Then we are in the sky. Above the eagles. Like them.'

She glanced at the factor. He looked concerned, and she imagined that he was signalling to her not to accept. But what business was it of his if she chose to go off with Carlo in his sea-plane? She frowned at the factor, who looked away in his embarrassment. When you lived so close to somebody, month in, month out, you sometimes forgot what the boundaries were. A factor would normally never tell his principal what he or she could do; but might still make a suggestion, as one would to a friend.

'I have every confidence in our guest,' she said, and smiled.

The factor did not meet her gaze. He thought that it would be madness to go for a ride in the plane. How could she say that she had every confidence in a man whom she had met barely a few hours ago? He would not say that – not just yet.

11

The next morning the ghillie announced that it would be best to wait until late afternoon before going out on the hill.

'The deer are coming off the hill,' he said. 'One or two big stags. But not just yet. If we go up there we might discourage them. We'll go this afternoon.'

Carlo listened. 'In that case, we can go for a spin.'

The factor looked at him half-mockingly. 'A spin. Planes go into a spin. Then ...'

Carlo said nothing. He did not grasp what was said; an understanding of a language may be less extensive than apparent fluency suggests.

The factor looked at her and shook his head. 'It could turn nasty. What if the water gets choppy? Where will you land? Fly all the way down to Lochaline?'

She sought to reassure him. 'I'm not worried, Jimmy. I'm really not.'

12

Carlo rowed them out in the ghillie's old rowing boat. The surface of the loch was flat; so calm that the hills were reflected with virtually no distortion. There were purples, greens, and above them the light blue, almost a white, of the sky.

'Look,' said Carlo. 'Scotland is in the water.'

It struck her as a strange way of putting it. Scotland in the water.

She clambered out of the boat and onto one of the plane's floats. Her weight made the plane rock; he steadied it, reaching up from the boat to hold on to one of the wings.

'You're quite safe,' he called out. 'Get in.'

She struggled to open the door while he fastened the rowing boat to the mooring buoy. Then he loosened the line attaching the plane; the aircraft would not drift in these conditions. He joined her in the cockpit of the plane. It was very small, she thought, and her knees were pressed against the instruments.

'Don't worry about that,' he said. 'Most of them don't work anyway. They do nothing.'

She laughed at that, but later, as the plane taxied along the loch, the floats bumping and thudding as it gained speed, she wondered how well it was maintained – this bundle of ageing machinery to which she was entrusting her life. She glanced sideways at her pilot; he was unconcerned, relaxed, his hands light upon the controls, as one would hold the top of a walking stick on a casual stroll.

13

From above, she saw the proper shape of the sea loch for the first time. It had been her home for so many years, but she had not seen before that it was shaped like a distended sock. And the sky was larger, too, than she had ever imagined it could be, and shaped differently. It was a bowl, above and around her; she was within it and of it. She craned her neck to look down. There was her house, and the factor's house, and the sheep on the hill like tiny grey stones.

He suddenly brought the nose of the aircraft up, so that the sky was in front of them. The engine shuddered as it fought more directly with gravity. Then for a moment the plane seemed to hang quite still before it flipped over on its back and dived down towards the loch below.

She screamed. It was not a scream of fear, though; rather it was one of exhilaration. She had last screamed in this way when, as a child, she had been taken to a fun fair outside Edinburgh and had been unprepared for the violence of one of the rides.

14

The factor was waiting on the shore when they landed. He saw that her eyes were moist, and he immediately stepped forward to put his arm about her. He glared at the Italian, who was surprised by the hostility in his expression.

He took her aside. 'You must be—'

'No, I'm fine. It was immensely exciting. I've never experienced anything like it before. Never.'

The factor shook his head in disbelief. 'I thought you were going to end up in the loch.' He turned to Carlo. 'Show-off,' he muttered, as if in jest, but really meaning it.

'Thank you,' said the Italian. He had misread the comment as a compliment.

15

The Italian shot a stag that afternoon. She refused to look at it, as it came down the hillside on the broad back of one of the ponies. She watched from her window, though, as Carlo spoke to the ghillie. He was gesticulating about something; some argument was taking place, or perhaps just a discussion.

That evening she had dinner with Carlo in the house. He told her about his life. He was the owner of a cheese factory near Reggio Emilia. 'It is not a town that many people visit. But it suits me very well. I have a villa in the countryside. That is where we keep the special cows who make our cheese. Parmigiano-Reggiano. We have been making it since the thirteenth century.'

She smiled. 'The thirteenth century. What were we doing in the thirteenth century? Fighting with one another, I suppose. Raiding cattle.'

He spread his hands. 'Everyone finds the way of life that suits them.'

'Do you think so?' she asked. 'But it's strange, isn't it, how we are all caught up in not only our own little history, but the history of others. Of parents, grandparents. Of places. All this history. And it ties us down.'

He shrugged. 'Maybe. But let's talk about what is to come, not the past. Would you like to come to Italy? I could show you.'

She did not know what to say. Was this a question that had been asked out of mere politeness, or was it a real invitation? She had no idea as to whether Carlo was married; she saw no ring, but that did not mean anything.

'Oh.'

'I mean it,' he said. 'I could show you. It is very beautiful where I live. We could see other places too. Venice. I have an aunt there. Diamantina. She is a great character.'

16

That night she had a confused dream. She was in Italy, but not quite in Italy. She was sitting with a woman called

Diamantina in a café, but not quite in a café. There was cheese on a plate before her. Diamantina was telling her a story about her youth. She was conscious of an atmosphere of love that suffused the dream, transformed it into a vision.

17

The next morning Carlo discovered that his plane had sunk. The floats had failed for some reason and let in water. The small green plane had settled in the water and then gently rocked down to the bottom of the loch, forty feet below.

The ghillie thought he saw it, or part of it, the glint of metal far below in the clear green water of the loch. 'That's an awful thing to happen,' he said. 'I don't see how ...'

'Metal fatigue,' said the factor.

The Italian held his gaze.

'I'm so sorry about your little plane,' she said. 'Mr Macgregor's boat has this crane thing – a sort of boom. He is very resourceful when it comes to fishing things out of the water.'

Carlo seemed not to be worried. 'We should not become too attached to machinery,' he said. 'Nor to places, I suppose. Both can be taken away from us like that.'

He clicked his fingers to illustrate the temporary nature of the world.

18

She prepared a picnic for him that day, which they ate at a place that she liked, high on the hillside above the house, near a burn. From there they could see the dark blue swirl of the Atlantic coming in round the point to the south. The sun was on the water; the air was still.

The Tipping Point

HELEN SIMPSON's first collection of short stories, *Four Bare Legs in a Bed* (1990), won the *Sunday Times* Young Writer of the Year Award. There followed *Dear George, Hey Yeah Right Get a Life* (winner of the Hawthornden Award) and *Constitutional*. Her fifth collection of stories, *In Flight Entertainment*, will be published in 2009 and includes 'The Tipping Point'. She lives in London with her husband and two children.

LOOK AT THAT SKY. It's almost sitting on the windscreen. Whose idea was it to hold the Summer School up in the wilds this year? I know my sweet Americans would follow me to the ends of the earth for my thoughts on the Bard; and I know Stratford venues are stratospheric these days. But all this way to study the Scottish play *in situ* smacks of desperation. If ever a sky looked daggers, this is it.

I was quite looking forward to the drive, actually. Impossible to get lost, my esteemed colleague Malkie MacNeil told me; just follow the A82 all the way and enjoy the scenery, the mountains, best in the world blah blah. So I left Glasgow reasonably bright and hopeful this morning after a dish of porridge, up along Loch Lomond, and the light has drained steadily away through Tarbet, Ardlui, Tyndrum, until I realise that it's eleven in the morning on the fifth of August and I've got to turn on the headlights. Storm clouds over Glen Coe. 'The cloud-capp'd Towers, the gorgeous Palaces.' Not really. More like a celestial housing estate.

Alright, let's have something suitably gloomy in the way of music. Here we are. *Winterreise* with Dietrich Fischer-Dieskau and his manly baritone. No finer example of the pathetic fallacy than Schubert's *Winterreise*. 'What's that when it's at home, Dr Beauman?' That is the reading of one's own emotion into external nature, child. I still cannot believe that I, confirmed commitmentphobe, have been cast as the rejected lover, ignominiously dumped like some soppy First Year.

Nun ist die Welt so trübe, der Weg gehüllt in Schnee. My German may not be fluent but it's become more than passable in the last year. You'd allow that, Angelika? Now the world is so bleak, the path shrouded in snow. *Schnee.*

It was immediate. As soon as we first clapped eyes on each other etcetera. But, joking apart, it was. I was over in Munich to give my paper on *Milton's Comus; the Masque Form as Debate and Celebration,* mainly because I wanted to check out the painted rococo Cuvilliés-Theater – crimson, ivory and gold – on Residenzstrasse. I needed it for my chapter on European Court Theatre, for the book which now bears your name as dedicatee.

You were in charge of that conference, Head of Arts Admin for all the participating institutions that week. Once it was over we went back to your flat in Cologne. Jens was staying with his grandmother as luck would have it. Beautiful Angelika, with your fierce pale eagle eyes and beaming smile. I remember capering round your bed like a satyr after you'd given me the first of your ecological curtain lectures. I was quoting *Comus* at you to shut you up:

Wherefore did nature pour her bounties forth
With such a full and unwithdrawing hand,
Covering the earth with odours, fruits and flocks,
Thronging the seas with spawn innumerable,
But all to please and sate the curious taste?

I was proud and stout and gleeful in the presence of your angularity. It felt like a challenge. Heaping you with good things became part of that. I filled your austere kitchen with delicacies, though that wasn't easy as you are of course vegan.

'Enough is enough,' you said, pushing me away.

'You can never have enough,' I laughed. 'Didn't you know that?'

'Not so. I have.'

Ich will den Boden küssen / durdringen Eis und Schnee / mit meinen heißen Tränen. Schnee again. I want to kiss the ground, to pierce the ice and snow with my hot tears. Yes, well.

Romanticism was your besetting sin, Angelika; your quasi-mystical accusatory ecospeak about the planet. Whereas my line is, if it's going to happen, it's going to happen – I don't see how anything mankind does can impose change on overwhelming natural phenomena like hurricanes and tsunamis. We resemble those small frail figures in a painting by Caspar David Friedrich, dwarfed by the immensity of nature. You took me to see his great painting *Das Eismeer* in the Hamburger Kunsthalle, jagged ice floes in a seascape beyond hope; and you used it as a jumping-off point to harangue me about the collapse of the Larsen B ice shelf. My clever intense passionate Angelika, so quick to imagine the worst, and so capable of anguish; you wept like a red-eyed banshee when you gave me the push.

An ominous cloudscape, this, great weightless barricades of cumulonimbus blocking the light. I can't see another car or any sign of humanity. Once out of this miserable valley, I'll stop for petrol in Ballachulish. Then it's on up past Loch Linnhe, Loch Lochy, Loch Oich, Loch Ness, and I'll be there. Inverness. What's done is done. Halfway through the week there's a day trip planned to Cawdor Castle, where Duncan doubtless shakes his gory locks on mugs and mousemats all over the gift shop.

So then I applied for a peripatetic fellowship at the University of Cologne, and got it. I brushed up my Schiller.

I wrote a well-received paper on Gotthold Lessing's *Minna von Barnhelm* and gave a seminar on Ödön von Horváth, the wandering playwright who all his life was terrified of being struck by lightning and then, during a Parisian thunderstorm, took shelter beneath a tree on the Champs-Elysées and was killed by a falling branch. Let that be a warning to you, Angelika: you can worry too much.

We were very happy, you and me and Jens. He's unusually thoughtful and scrupulous, that boy; like his mother. They had their annual day of atonement at his school while I was over, when the children are instructed to consider the guilt of their militaristic forefathers in the last century. That was the night he had an asthma attack and we ended up in Casualty. Cue copious lectures from you on air quality, of course.

And here's the rain, driving against the windscreen with a violence fit to crack it. It's almost comic, this journey, the menace of those massed clouds, the grey-green gloom. Nor do I have a residual belief that rain is in any way cleansing or purgative. No, no. As you so painstakingly taught me, Angelika, our sins of pollution lock into the clouds and come down as acid rain. Hence *Waldsterben*, or forest death; and from *Waldsterben* you would effortlessly segue into flash floods, storm surge, wildfire, drought, and on to carbon sequestration. You were not the only one. You and your friends discussed these things for hours, organising petitions, marching here and there. Your activism made my English students look like solipsistic children, their political concerns stretching with some effort to top-up fees and back down again to the price of hair straighteners.

You were in a constant state of alarm. I wanted you to talk about me, about you and me, but the apocalyptic zeitgeist intruded.

Darling, shall we go for a swim? No, my love, for the oceans have warmed up and turned acidic. All plankton is doomed and, by association, all fish and other swimmers. Sweetheart, what can I do to melt your heart? Nothing, for you are indifferent to the ice albedo feedback; you are unconcerned that the planet's shield of snow, which reflects heat back into space, is defrosting. That our world grows dangerously green and brown, absorbing more heat than ever before, leaves you cold.

My own dear heart, let's make a happy future for ourselves, for you and me and Jens. How can that be when the world is melting and you don't care? How can we be *gemütlich* together in the knowledge that the twin poles of the world are dissolving, that permafrost is no longer permanent and will unloose vast clouds of methane gas to extinguish us all?

You did love me. You told me so. *Ich liebe dich.*

Then came your ultimatum. We couldn't go on seeing each other like this. Yes, you loved my flying visits, you loved being with me. But no, you could not bear it that our love was sustained at the expense of the future. By making it dependent on cut-price flights we were doing the single worst possible thing in our power as private individuals to harm the planet.

'Love miles,' I countered, morally righteous, fighting fire with fire.

'Selfish miles,' you retorted. 'We are destroying other people's lives when we do this.' Very truthful and severe you are, Angelika; very hard on yourself as well as others.

Time for a change of CD. More Schubert lieder, I think, but let's drop Fischer-Dieskau. He's a tad heavy-hearted for Scotland, a bit of a dampener where it's already damp enough. Ah, Gérard Souzay, he's my man. Rather an eccentric choice, but my father used to listen to him and I cottoned on to what he admired. A great voice, fresh, rich, essentially baritonal but keener on beauty than usual. Let's skip *Der Jüngling und der Tod*, though. OK, here comes the Erlking. There's a boy here, too, riding on horseback through the night with his father, holding close to his father. Oh, it's a brilliant micro-opera, this song, one voice singing four parts – narrator, father, boy and the lethal wheedling Erlking. I'd forgotten how boldly elliptical it is, and how infectious the boy's terror – *Mein Vater, mein Vater, und hörest du nicht / Was Erlenkönig mir leise verspricht?* My father, my father, and don't you hear/ the Erlking whispering promises to me? But his father can't hear anything, can't see anything, only the wind and the trees.

I used to start laughing uncontrollably at this point, which annoyed *my* father, who was trying to listen; but it appealed to my puerile sense of humour – *Vater* as farter.

Mein Vater, mein Vater, jetzt fasst er mich an!
Erlkönig hat mir ein Leids getan!

My father, my father, now he is taking hold of me! The Erlking has hurt me! And by the time the father has reached home the boy lies dead in his arms. *Tot.*

Listen, Angelika. You make my blood boil. What possible difference can it make whether I get on a plane or not? The plane will take off regardless. Why don't you concentrate your energies on all those herds of farting cattle, eh? All those cows and sheep farting and belching. Then after that you could get the rainforests under control! The blazing forests! You don't want me.

It's stopped raining at last. I can see ahead again, the air is clearer now. A truly theatrical spectacle, this sky, with its constant changes of scene. I couldn't do it in the end. I wanted tenure, sure, but I was being asked to give up too much. The world. The world well lost? No. No, no, not even for you, Angelika.

In September I'm attending a weekend conference on Performance Art at the University of Uppsala in Sweden. I'm not going by coach. There's a seminar on *Sturm und Drang* in Tokyo this autumn, as well as my Cardiff-based sister's wedding party in Seville. After that there's an invitation to the Sydney Festival to promote my new book, and the usual theatre conference at Berkeley in spring. All paid for, of course, except the return ticket to Seville, which cost me precisely £11 – just about manageable even on an academic's meagre stipend.

You used to have to join the Foreign Office if you wanted to travel on anything like this scale. Now everybody's at it. The budget airlines arrived and life changed overnight.

Sorry, but it's true. The world's our sweetshop. We've got used to it, we want it; there's no going back.

The downside is, I lost my love. She followed through. And how. She caused us both enormous pain. Ah, come on! For all I know she's got back together with that little dramaturg from Bremen, the one with the tiny hands and feet. So?

Look at those schmaltzy sunbeams backlighting the big grey cloud. Perfect scenery for the arrival of a deus ex machina. 'What's that when it's at home, Dr Beauman?'

A far-fetched plot device to make everything alright again, my dear. There's Ballachulish in the distance. A painted god in a cardboard chariot. An unlikely happy ending, in other words.

Suddenly
Doctor Cox

DBC PIERRE was born in South Australia in 1961 but grew up in Mexico ('my soul has a Mexican passport'). He moved to Leitrim, Ireland, in 2001, after completing his Booker Prize winning novel, *Vernon God Little*. It was followed by *Ludmilla's Broken English* (2006). DBC Pierrre is a nom-de-plume: the first part stands for 'Dirty But Clean' while 'Pierre' was a childhood nickname from a cartoon character of that name.

DRIVING TO WORK I SAW the most beautiful roadkill. It was a carpet of iridescent butterflies, squashed but flashing on the highway, as if concrete had worn thin over a seam of priceless opal. Wings twitched and glinted in the heat, spurring that human compulsion to stop and urgently gather treasures. But it was a frustrated compulsion. Under the sparkle were only dead insects. Like suicide-butterflies they swarmed from the jungle to die under mini-vans that throbbed drum and bass music; and when the traffic was light, to lie wavering in gentle reggaes that wafted down the mountains like fog. Even in death the butterflies were delicate and stunning. What a baroque start to a day, to a season, this emperor's carpet of beauty and needless death; if any death can be needless, or beautiful. I tried not to hit the butterflies with the car but it was impossible; I swerved and slalomed in vain. And the drive made me ponder: whatever made the creatures shine in life was still active after death.

Beauty had survived them, and in a strange way was even framed and made meaningful by their deaths. At any rate I will never forget them, nor the feelings and philosophies I had to suddenly deal with.

This was my first day of work in Trinidad. When I arrived at my new office I found that a young man lived in the dirt under the building. He was black, with doll's eyes and a jutting, almost hanging lower lip. I discovered he was there when a colleague went to a particular spot on the office floor and stamped on it hard.

'Cox,' he explained.

After a few moments a man shuffled into the office. He was glazed with sleep, and looked like he'd slept in his clothes. David Cox was his name. His fly was open. He shuffled because his workboots had no laces. In a hangdog manner he took instructions from the colleague for an errand. His voice lacked the full twang and lilt of Trinidad, but had a drawl that tapered to quiet at the end of his words, making them somehow sad. He also mushed them in the way of Sean Connery. Cox shuffled away on his errand, probably to find food, and I watched his head weave past the tinted windows and up the road into Port of Spain. Then sunshine smacked the Gulf of Paria, opposite our building, and swallowed him up in a gleam. Mangroves, manatees and mud-crabs must have stirred

– in the languid haze you didn't have to see them to know they were there.

I first came to Trinidad for a cricket match. Now it was my first day of work in an air-conditioned office with a man living under it. Well, don't ask me how one thing led to the other. Suddenly I was among colleagues, not many more than a dozen, who were a teeming sample of the island's bloods: Afro-Caribbean, East Indian, Syrian, French Creole, Anglo and Chinese. Their natures were so bright that my steepest learning didn't come from the work we were meant to do together in the office, but from catching up with local patois, with wining and grinning and liming, with doubles and roti and parlour-juice, with macajuels, mapipires and pommes-cythere, with play-whe and soca and chutney and parang. And threaded between it all, between the island's scent of intimate sweat and the bating of breath in case a boa constrictor should thud from the trees – I gradually learned more about the man under the building.

'He fast,' someone told me. 'Watch out.'

David Cox would present himself in the office most mornings wearing some variation on a sheepish face. Understandable, I thought, if somebody stomps floorboards over your sleeping head. Apparently he was the building's security guard, though he was absent most hours of the day, and seemed also to roam at night. One morning, while Cox shuffled about the office, a colleague grinned and told me there had only been two break-ins during his tenure – and Cox had committed them both.

In the background Cox's eyes fell; his shuffle grew awkward. I heard him click his tongue.

David Cox had been a street boy before mysteriously fetching up at our building. At first he had been allowed to spend his nights indoors; but after something went missing one night, he was banished outside. Our wooden single-storey building was raised off the ground, with a planked skirt around its base that hid the pillars and foundations. The front of the office faced a busy road along the gulf, but at its side was a residential cul-de-sac partly shaded by the building's coconut palm, and with an exotic ruin across the road that dated back to the coup d'état, now fully reclaimed by lush foliage, with flowers, and arctic-white herons that posed in the sun; and behind the office, through a froth of hibiscus and bougainvillea, a narrow alley ran between the building and the neighbour's fence. There David Cox had scraped a hole under the planks, and fashioned a nest from old clothes.

Cox never seemed to wear the same outfit twice. Over time his fashions showed that he was a man of drifting spirit; his accuracy to good taste had a margin of surprise in every direction. Some days he would suddenly appear in an old lady's gardening hat, other days in the garb of a pimp, or a child, or a ramshackle country gent. I was told all his clothes came from a charity bin. He had the biggest wardrobe in Trinidad, and it doubled as his bed.

'Good morning sir, I'll carry your bag.' He would appear out of nowhere when I stepped from the car in the morning.

'Thanks, Cox. I can carry it. And never mind "sir" – it's only me.'

'Yes sir mister sir.'

There was a creeping feeling on the island, as in many post-colonial places, that every good turn done for you was a token soon to be redeemed against cash. With this in mind, and with everything I had been told about Cox, I tried to keep a cordial distance at first.

'Sir, mister sir sir—'

'Cox,' – I stopped to face him once under the coconut tree – 'you're not my servant.'

A sparkle came to his eye. 'Just testing.'

As the weeks unfolded I saw that Cox was a man on the move, with a quick intelligence and a child's candour. There came a time when I started staying back late in the office, and, as he grew used to me being there, he also came around. After a while two things would happen at night: at a certain time, quite late, a shadowy car would pull up outside. Figures would come to the door and hand me foam containers of food and drink. And soon after, Cox would darken the door and come in for the food. We chatted, and he made himself coffee, or used the bathroom. The building's masters didn't want him coming in at night, but he was good with me, and had a good mind; so after a while we grew familiar.

'Lend me fifty dollars,' he would say.

'I'll lend you the sharp end of a pineapple.'

'I was only joking.'

'The sharp end of a pineapple, I say.'

'What! I was only joking!'

'Good.'

'But do you have ten? I'll pay you back.'

And so it went with Cox, who could mount vast philosophical structures to achieve his ends: 'But listen to me,' he might say, 'have you, in your life, given a total of more than ten dollars to beggars?'

'Of course.'

'But you never saw that money, nor probably the beggars, ever again, right? So here, on the one hand, you're capable of throwing money clean away into the ether; and on the other, of resisting to lend to a sort of colleague who you know you'll see every day, and whose life you can make hell until you get paid.'

'Cox – it's a beg. A high-functioning beg, because you know I don't want to make your life hell. You're trading on my sympathies.'

'What! Do I look like a beggar? Like a man who would trade on sympathies?' His arms would fly in outrage.

'Yes.'

'Well. Maybe a technical beg.'

'And look, don't enable that stereotype where I'm rich just because I came over from England, or owe you in a cultural sense because your poverty derives from a colonial past. Everyone has their roll of dice in life – I get paid on the same day as you, by the same people, and until then am in the same relative condition.'

'Wow.' His lip would fall back to a resting hang. 'Like you really got out the wrong side of the bed this morning. Wow.'

I would turn my eyes on him.

'Wow.' He would shuffle away in his laceless boots. 'Like – at least you *have* a bed. At least you *have*—'

'Cox – I'll give you five dollars. Okay? *Give* them to you.'

'No, no,' he would dismiss me over his shoulder. 'Far be it from me to jeopardise the harmony of our interrelationship.' Cox really did have a golden tongue, who knows from where.

'Coxy – we're starting to sound like an old married couple. Just take the five.'

'Yes mister sir thank you sir.'

'And don't be like that.'

'Okay but I'll pay you back.'

'You don't have to; that's the idea.'

'But only a *beggar* wouldn't pay it back, only a *beggar*—'

And so gently I joined Cox's orbit of support, delighting as he did in our philosophical charades. We alternated the roles of mentor and pupil; he with the wiles of the streets, and me with the overworld that was inexplicably out of his reach. One day, for instance, he watched me take a generous stance with a colleague, but get landed with an hour's extra work as a result.

He sidled up to me afterwards. 'You need to master mood swings.'

I looked up from my desk.

'Don't be so predictable. Get a reputation for moodiness and nobody will hit on you for favours.' He winked and shuffled away.

Then there came a season when Cox started coming in with an old briefcase full of documents. One day he asked if I could read one to him. I wasn't sure if it was because he thought I would find the paper interesting – but it turned out that he couldn't read or write. He was too proud or too embarrassed to ask anyone else. Alongside a small kitchen area in our office there was a cubby with table and chairs, and Cox would sit there with the briefcase of papers, shuf-fling them, sometimes pacing importantly back and forth, muttering to himself. It was sad to watch. He had a shine that would have taken him anywhere in life, given only the most basic chances. Instead his faculties were turned to ek-ing small wins on the streets, among equals in cunning who hadn't half his humanity.

The beggars in the capital were the best talkers I'd ever seen, and each had a trademark style: there was the grand supplicant with the Moses beard who would approach reaching out like a toddler and whimpering, 'My lord, my lord,' in a tragic falsetto. There was a snappy beggar outside a pub who would sing for a burger, and Fat Beggar, a portly chancer who would saunter past busy food stands and say to a patron: 'Give me ten dollars.' If they said no, he would demand three breakfasts. Threats as bright as parrots always flocked around Fat Beggar: 'Ten dollars? I'll crack you down with the door of this car,' etcetera. There was also the well-spoken white man who claimed to be Hitler's brother, and gave creditable dissertations on the fall of the Reich. And there were genuine ragamuffins, who never spoke but sim-ply scavenged in the gutters of the town – some could only walk on all fours. And precisely where Cox roamed in this sweltering arena, or what he really did, was a mystery to everyone.

One day I squeezed through the hibiscus behind the building to see where he lived. There were cables running over the fence.

Cox had power. He had cable TV in his burrow. I didn't have a TV in my house. But Cox had cable in the dirt. He had rigged a line from a pole on the street. The bushes at the back of the building would flicker colours in the night.

Some time after seeing this I noted Cox was more anxious, and more attentive to his errands, in a bumbling sort of way. He forgot about his case of important papers for a time. Then I heard that his television was gone. He had sold it to an old lady, under some crushing sudden debt.

'But how stupid he is,' someone told me. 'He only had it on hire purchase – Lord knows how he talked anyone into giving him credit. His tongue did its work that day. Now he sold it for less than he owes the shop, and he already spent the money he sold it for.'

Cox sharpened his wits as this new weight bore down. The energy of miracles came to him, as it can to certain people whose hopes and pressures blaze persistently inside them. One night after colleagues finished work they sent him up the road to buy beers. Cox went for the beers, and came running back with the bottles; but he was careless crossing the avenue to the office. A car hit him. It tossed him into the air, and tossed the beers up with him.

Cox survived to limp away. And he caught the beers. Not one was broken.

A legend was born in Port of Spain.

Still, and it's probably in the nature of living legends, the period wasn't all plain sailing for Cox. It saw him taking a more vigorous interest in being a security guard, which is a job also calling for steady judgment. Now he fancied himself Chief of Security. The nights I was there he more noticeably prowled outside, coming to the door every so often to check on me. He lurked, those days, and his eyes shifted suspiciously left and right like a secret agent. When I finished at night I would find him prowling by the door; he would hold up a hand while he scanned the shadows for villains, before waving me to my car.

This was his spirit the night he spied a figure on the roof of a nearby building. Cox sprang into action, assembling a posse of vagrants to rout the intruder, who tried every ruse to dissuade them. With sticks and projectiles they managed to dislodge the man from his perch, and gave him a thorough pasting on the ground.

But when the police came the man was identified as the security guard for that building.

The posse vanished into the shadows. Cox went to jail, and our masters didn't get there to bail him out for at least another day due to laughter.

After this Cox drifted back to his shuffling self, coming to the office at night with important paperwork that he couldn't read, scrutinising and sorting it with momentous frowns, grunts and sighs. He shaved his hair close, and started wearing granny-glasses he had found somewhere or other. Suddenly Doctor Cox, with his glasses, and his case of papers. Not long after this next of his little lives began, I saw him by the avenue with a mobile phone. He paced up and down having earnest conversations, eyes reacting this way and that behind his glasses. Cox didn't want to show us his new phone, but I found it one night and saw it was a rubber toy. One that squeaked when you squeezed it. It also had a little antenna that went up and down.

At his table in the cubby, next to his papers, he sometimes extended the antenna to listen for incoming calls. One time he handled the phone too roughly and it squeaked. He flinched, peering around to see if we'd heard.

After that it stayed in the case.

Everyone reckoned that Cox was about twenty-three years old. He actually carried a birth certificate in his pocket, like a passport, and it had his mother's name. But nobody had put his name, or date of birth.

Cox's mother was long dead.

One night I watched him through the window as he sat with a clean, proper-looking girl. She had come from a workplace, in her suit, and Cox had spruced himself up to meet her in dazzling white trousers. They sat on the ledge under the coconut tree. It was Cox's first date. All he felt he could offer the young woman was a convincing panto-mime of worth. I watched thinking it was perhaps all any of us can offer. Cox frowned and smiled and frowned, and his hands masterfully framed notions and surprises for the girl. Occasionally he stepped away to take a call on his phone. I lurked in the dark of the window hoping the thing didn't squeak.

As I began to lock up for the night, he hurried to meet me on the steps. When Cox was nervous or frightened his eyes grew round, and he clenched his teeth so that you could see them clenched.

'Mister sir, sir ...'

'Don't worry,' I said. And passing the girl on my way to the car: 'See you tomorrow, Doctor Cox.'

The girl didn't come around again; I suspected she would have liked to, but Cox only had the ledge under the coconut tree to entertain her. He had illuminated what might have been, and that was all he felt he could ask of life. Plus the phone would've eventually squeaked.

He went back to his paperwork at night, shuffling and sorting it in and out of his case. He used to ask if I had any official-looking correspondence I could give him for his collection. But after reading the occasional letter for Cox I noticed some were beginning to arrive addressed to him. They were letters from businesses and civic groups; statements of support for some kind of charity.

Cox had founded a charity. With his glasses and briefcase, and perhaps with his phone, he had been trawling the town garnering support for a foundation for poor children and orphans. Businesses were offering to host bins on their premises where people could leave Christmas gifts. Then at Christmas Cox would deliver all the gifts to the nation's children in care.

As this dawned on we colleagues, that Cox's battered case had begun to contain real work, a cry rang out one day from the director's office.

Cox was on television. He was on television with Miss Universe.

Trinidad and Tobago and her mainland neighbour Venezuela have more than their fair share of Miss Worlds and Miss Universes; one of the most recent at that time was Trinidadian. Here she was with him. He wore his glasses. They laughed together. Later that afternoon he passed by the office grinning, to a hail of jeers and taunts, then went out to find prostitutes for some Chinese seamen off a rusty freighter in return for a few dollars. After that he stole some coconuts from our office tree, was discovered and took a tongue-lashing for it; then retired to his hole under the building. That was Cox's day in the sun.

When Christmas came, our office became a depot and command centre for the distribution of gifts. Things had looked up for Cox, and our nights at the office developed a routine – but, being Cox, this was soon disrupted. I opened the door to his rattling one night, and he came in to ask if he could use the phone. I let him in, and paid little attention to his phone conversation. But suddenly – and strangely for the time of night – a second phone line started to ring. I picked it up on another receiver, and it was our boss calling from home. He demanded to know how Cox came to be using the office phone.

Cox had called a radio phone-in show, and among its listeners was the boss. It spelt the end of Cox's evenings in the office. Carnival season approached, and the twin island republic became a whirl. Carnival was a prime season for Cox and his street cronies as the island filled with newcomers, and the streets were awash with flesh and beer and rum. Occasionally his face would appear like a light bulb in this place or that – at the back of some of the most select parties, or on a carnival float, or running with packs of tourists. After that, Carnival hangover seemed to last months, and the office was slow to return to routine.

When I next saw Cox he seemed to have mange growing on his skin. And lumps had appeared in his neck. The mysterious car still delivered him food most nights, but it went uneaten more often than not.

I heard that Cox had AIDS.

He had befriended a tourist, one Carnival a few years earlier, when he was a teenager. They ended up at the tourist's hotel. I never discovered if the tourist was male or female; if the sex had been consensual or sold. When you knew Cox it was as shattering a thought as a child abduction. Because David Cox wasn't of the truly wasted street crowd. He never took drugs, nor dealt them. He giggled like a little girl when we goaded him into a half a bottle of beer one night in the office.

It transpired that Cox had been diagnosed some time ago, and had since developed full-blown AIDS. One of my colleagues had doctors in his family, and Cox was treated for free.

But his lip hung lower than ever, and he started to dribble. He began to lose his height and build, and his skin lost its shine. Still he rallied from time to time. Occasionally the young Doctor Cox would emerge with his spectacles, and his crucial business dealings. But Cox knew he was sick.

He asked me one night if I thought there was anything after death.

The shadowy car that delivered his supper turned out to be from one of the finest restaurants, not far around the corner. It was run by a pair of formidable women who had let themselves be tangled in Cox's net of charm. As he slowed and grew more dazed, and as we watched the glands on his neck swell, and his body show more bones, a quiet circuit of friendship showed itself around him – the restaurant, the doctor, the bosses at the office. Without fanfare his needs were catered to by souls who were touched by him.

When Cox was suddenly taken to the Accident and Emergency department, my colleague Kirtlee and I donned suit jackets and strode into Port of Spain General Hospital to find him. He was on a large ward.

'It's nothing,' he said. 'Just a cough. Tell them I'm coming back.'

He did come back for a while – but he disappeared again, this time to a facility on a lush mountainside, with a view over all the land. I was leaving the island for a few weeks, and before I left I made the journey to find him. He was on a bed next to a prisoner in chains.

Cox spread out his hands and grinned his terrified grin, as if acknowledging a dark and colossal joke. I brought him treats, and a wallet with some pieces of official paperwork. But seeing him there, wide-eyed with his situation, I knew his spirit had flowered, his time had come and gone. I hugged him, and told him to wait for me; I would bring him something back from my travels.

But Cox couldn't wait.

He told his last visitors that I was coming back. But it was from them I heard on the phone that he was dead. They buried him at La Peyrouse cemetery; his friends came from the office, from the restaurant, and apparently an unexpected number from out of the woodwork of gingerbread houses and palms and shadows. I don't know if Miss Universe was there; but it doesn't matter.

Mist hung over Port of Spain when I got back. It was butterfly season again. The highway was strewn with needless victims; all dead, but flashing fire and colour from where they lay.

Vanish

AL KENNEDY (born Dundee, 1965) writes novels, short stories and non-fiction; drama for radio, TV and stage; teaches creative writing at the University of Warwick; and performs as a stand-up comedian at the Edinburgh Fringe, comedy clubs and literary festivals. Her last novel, *Day*, won the 2008 Costa Book of the Year Award. She lives in Glasgow. 'Vanish' is a new story from her forthcoming collection, *What Becomes*.

IT HAD BEEN HER FAULT, ENTIRELY. Dee's fault – the whole bloody evening.

Which, to be truthful, made him slightly glad – it was, after all, three months since she had hurt him a new way. Tonight, in her undoubted absence, she was letting Paul feel reconnected, touched.

He'd bought the tickets for her just before they'd split, intending to give her a treat – an almost-birthday treat – 19th October and a trip to the West End, a fairly pricey dinner first and then off to a show. 19th October meant pretending she was a late Libra instead of an early Scorpio – as if that mattered a toss and would in any way have made her not a car crash as a person. Paul didn't even read horoscopes, she was the one who read horoscopes, he thought they were total shit. Probably, if he checked somewhere, consulted a website, it would be set down as axiomatic that early Scorpios were also total shit. But at that point he'd been

63

trying for her, he'd been keeping the faith and imagining she would come through and turn out to be – what? Sane? Undamaged? Undamaging? – he could no longer be bothered to guess.

For the usual reasons, he'd gone the extra mile again, got hold of tickets before the place sold out and reserved them two seats in their future, side by side and near the front without being too close, because that could get scary. This magician bloke was somebody she'd talked about – she'd said he was really good – and there was bugger all she thought was really good on anything like a consistent basis – himself included – and the guy was going to be in London for a limited engagement, which sounded exclusive, sounded right – so everything should have worked out fine.

Everything might have worked out fine.

She could have enjoyed it.

The chances of that happening had been quite high.

But then she'd done a runner, she'd ditched him, and this time it was clearly permanent.

And Dee hadn't even known about the tickets. This leaving a possibility that had swung away now and again from beneath Paul's feet: a trapdoor thought of her being in the theatre anyway; of their meeting in the foyer, on the stairs, in the stalls; his hope and fear interleaving, building up an uneven, uneasy stack.

I didn't see her, though. The whole evening I didn't see her. And I almost did look.

Frankly, I don't believe she'd have got it together enough to have come along. So why would I see her? How could I?

And I did look.

I did, in fact, very much look.

I stared so hard things went all cinematic – felt like I was the one who wasn't really here.

For a while, he'd assumed he would tear both the tickets up – or else ignore them until their relevance had faded.

And then, at the turn of the week, he'd decided he ought to enjoy the whole experience on his own, reclaim it. Naturally, he'd skip the dinner and the effort at romance. There wasn't another woman he could take – a substitute, stand-in, fresh start – it just so happened there was no one new to hand and that kind of thing would, in any case, only hurt him: he wasn't ready for it yet. Nevertheless, he'd been fully persuaded that he should set out for an evening of having fun.

Even if the chances of fun happening had been quite low.

He'd dressed nicely – best suit, a flashy tie which he'd regretted and had taken off almost at once – it was folded in his pocket now. For some reason he had forgotten that nothing made singleness worse than being well turned out.

If he could look good – and he did look pretty good, pretty easily – then his being not on the arm of a lovely escort was down to some deeper problem, an internal flaw.

Kind eyes, decent haircut, reliable mouth – somebody said that once: reliable mouth – but repeatedly bolloxed relationships, year after year. Must be broken where it doesn't show, then – something important about me gone missing, or else never arrived.

Dee – she said that I had a reliable mouth. So that probably doesn't count as true.

The other sodding ticket hadn't helped him: a leftover left with a leftover man, it had been a problem at once, already heavy in his pocket as he'd walked from the Underground, wandered up and eyed the posters hung outside the theatre: high monochrome repetitions of the magician's face.

He does have a reliable mouth.

Jesus, though, I don't even know what that would mean, really. Reliable, unreliable …

He has a mouth, that's all. Right where you'd expect. There it is, under his nose and over his chin – a mouth.

And he looks like a twat.

At least I don't do that.

The rhyme had made him smile – something from the Dr Seuss version of his life.

My girl let me down flat.

She is also a twat.

Paul had fingered the ticket and known he couldn't sit beside cold air, a ghost.

Which was why he'd turned up slightly early – this way he'd have some time to make enquiries in the queue.

'Hi. I have a spare ticket – do you want it?'

Clearing his throat and then being more assertive, 'Would you like this?'

Or maybe less assertive, 'Excuse me, would you like this?'

He'd been asking people who didn't have tickets, who wanted tickets, wanted them enough to come down here and wait in the hope of returns and who should have been pleased by an opportunity like this, an act of uncompromised generosity.

'Hi. Oh, you're together – this would be no use, then.' These ones had been bastards – a matching pair of self-satisfied bastards – covered with certainty, with the spring of the sex they were going to have tonight. 'No, I'll look for someone by themselves. I wouldn't want to break you up. I'm sorry.'

'Yes, it's a real ticket.'

'Good evening, I just wondered ...' He'd noticed he was starting to sweat. 'I have an extra ticket. There's nothing wrong with it. It's for quite a good seat – look.' The bloody thing had warped where he'd been touching it too long. 'That's a good seat.'

People had acted as if he were offering them a snake – which would always sound rude, now he thought about it, rude more than poisonous – *Hi, would you like my snake? I have this snake. Free snake. Free to a good home. Tired old snake seeks any deargodplease home that it can get.*

The best thing was truly, genuinely not to think of anything to do with sex at present. And maybe not ever again.

'Yes, you would be sitting next to me. Sorry.' Talking to women – had he, at any time, known how he should do that? 'Is that a problem? I'm not trying to … We'll forget about it, okay? … No, just forget about it. Really.' That's how you end up with the crazies – by never learning how you ought to reach the normal ones. 'You don't have to pay – I've paid. Sorry, that was me being ironic.'

Not that I expect you to appreciate that, or to find it amusing – but trust me – trust my perhaps reliable mouth, which I am not moving in case it shows you how I think – trust me while I do think, quite loudly, that I am laughing with my brain.

Leastways, maybe not laughing, but there is definitely something going on with me and with my brain. I think it is, perhaps, packing in advance of being gone.

'No, I don't want any money. The ticket's just no use to me … Well, if you want to pay me – then the price is written on it. Forty-five quid …. Yes, it is a lot, but then it is a good

seat ... Well, twenty quid isn't forty-five quid – that's like
... that's like you're ... I'd rather you didn't pay me. Either
nothing or the price, how would that be ...? I'm finding it
quite hard to understand why you don't opt for nothing ...
No, I wouldn't want to do that – it would hurt. But feel free
yourself.'

He'd never been aware of it before, but he did fairly often
grit his teeth.

Then again, he did fairly often have reason to.

'Ticket ...? Ticket?'

Eventually someone had tapped Paul on the shoulder –
this causing the foyer to ripple, contract, until he'd realised
he was looking into an unfamiliar manic smile. The person
smiling was slightly Goth-looking but clean, perhaps a student, had said his name was Simon and had asked if he could
have the spare seat. Paul released the ticket with a kind of
joy, or else at least a kind of satisfaction, because he was
working on the principle that if you wanted something you
should get it, you absolutely should, no matter who you
were or how ridiculous your need. This was the only magic
that might ever be worthwhile and should therefore be dem-
onstrated, encouraged to spread and thrive.

Thus far it had only affected Simon, of course: granting
him a seat he could not have afforded, even if he'd made
it to the head of the returns queue. The excitement of this

and his relative proximity to the stage, once they were both seated, made Simon chat a good deal, which Paul had not anticipated.

'This is beyond ... this is out of this world, is what this is. I just couldn't get off work, only then I did, only *then* I hadn't got a ticket, but I thought I'd have a go in any case, and *then* the bus broke down – I mean, what would be the probability of that particular bus breaking down on the way to *this* particular theatre? I had to run. From Regent's Street.'

Paul tried to calculate the probability of *his* breaking down while seated in the stalls of *this* particular theatre.

Simon, it was clear, had an over-large capacity for joy. 'He's amazing – The Great Man. They call him that – TGM. The initials. Did you know that? TGM. Not just us – his crew, his assistants, everyone *in the business*.'

It was ridiculous and unfair to imagine a person like Simon could unknowingly drain each remaining pleasure from those around him and leave them bereft. 'Do you know his work? Amazing guy. I've seen every show.' Even so, as Simon cast his hands about, shifted and stretched, Paul found himself taking great care that they didn't touch, didn't even brush shoulders, just to be sure that no draining could take place.

'The show before this? – *Mr Splitfoot?* – what a night. You see your first one and you always think he couldn't top it – but then he does. Excels himself. Over and over. *The lesson of excellence*. I had to go to Southport for him last January, can you believe it? *Southport*.'

Paul found he could believe in Southport but was primarily very happy to allow a new and gentle sliding thing to peel out across his mind and muffle him, make him almost sleepy, something close to sleepy: certainly opened, unsteady and soft. Simon was still talking – Paul could feel that – but the young man was also apparently dropping, further and further: falling with his sound beneath him into the wider and deeper, changeable din of individuals fitting themselves to an audience, becoming large, expecting. Their want teased and pressed at Paul's will and he tried to join them in it, to let go.

I don't know, though. I don't know.

The theatre was an old one: gilt- and rose-painted mouldings, candle brackets and layered galleries, rattling seats of golden plush and a chandelier there above them, holding up a monstrous threat of light.

I don't know.

Paul could appreciate the beauty of it, obviously – only he'd caught this other sense as well: that every charm was closing on him, folding down into a box, a mechanism already carefully set and working. He could almost hear it tick: cogging round to make him overly substantial, dense. And the ushers – it had seemed there were too many ushers, too many men dressed in black with unusual shoes who paced and watched and loitered casually, stood by the stage and by the entrances, moved with a purpose that made them another part of the elaborate, obscure machinery, of a building that had turned into a game. Paul didn't much like games – they made him lose. He didn't much like anyone who played them.

But it's just a performance. It's magic: that kind of game. If I think something's going on, then it probably might be, but there's no need to fret. It's nothing personal – it's just the magic, not anything wrong.

All of these people, packed in snug: they'd sent the air up to a blood heat and he'd liked that, which surprised him. And maybe this was how the game would work him – making him trapped and then offering release: the hope of joining something strange, the chance to be lost in the mind of a crowd, to evaporate. It had been, in a way, extremely welcoming.

I don't know, though.

Straight ahead had been the tall, naked dark of the stage. It stared at him, prepared.

Everyone else in here understands this. They're going to like it. They want to play.

I might not.

Then his morning fear had tickled unexpectedly in his chest – the creep of it as he would get out of bed and be alone – no one else there, nobody's belongings, only time in the flat and books he didn't read and DVDs of films he never really fancied watching and maybe this would be the way it was from hereon in – forever – maybe even with somebody there he was meant to love, trust, be loved by, maybe even then it would stay the same, had always been the same: himself locked somewhere airless, somewhere dead.

This evening is all of the things that she would like. Not me.

And he'd sat inside this thing that Dee would like while panic tilted in his neck and signalled a chill to the small of his back. He'd begun to wish hard that the lights would go down before he cried.

And then they did.

Like magic they did.

At the perfect point.

Exactly when another moment's wait would have toppled him, the colours had mellowed, the auditorium was withdrawn, was dimmed to exit signs and its private variety of night.

Evaporate now and nobody would see.

Nobody would stop me.

Or nobody would help.

There was no music.

Just breath – the audience noticing its nerves, stirring, giggling, settling again and holding.

Paul had shut his eyes. He'd inhaled the vaguely sweet and powdery warmth, the taste of attention, of other lives.

All right, then.

He'd tried to concentrate, to push and lift away from the restrictions of his skin, his skull. He was very tired, he'd realised, and had a great desire to be peaceful, uncluttered, unharried – to be not himself.

All right, then.

He'd begun to hear footsteps and, for an instant, they had seemed so natural, so much the start of an answer to soften his current need, that they might have been some internal phenomenon, an oddly convincing idea. Then they grew sharper: the hard, clear snap of leather soles that paced, perhaps climbing closer – yes, there was definitely a suggestion of stone steps winding upwards to the stage and raising an authoritative, measured tread. The sound was just a touch peculiar, amplified, treated.

All right.

Paul had unfolded his arms.

Yes.

He had let his hands rest easy on his lap. He'd blinked.

Yes.

He'd looked clear out into nowhere, into the free and shapeless deep of everything.

Do what you like.

And Paul had grinned as the footfalls halted, the proper pause extended and then the magician had walked out from the wings.

You do just precisely whatever you would like.

And The Great Man had been – *what?*

Sane?

Undamaged?

Undamaging? –

'Oh, what did you think, though. Really. I mean ...' When the final applause was done with, Simon had been not unexcited. 'First half – fantastic, but second half? Always a kicker.' He'd clutched at Paul's forearm, shaking it gently. 'What did you *think*? I didn't ask in the interval, I held back – didn't I hold back? – but *how* was *that?*' Simon had cornered him up at the top of the aisle, turning to peer back into the emptying theatre, the emptied stage. He'd pulled his free hand through his hair, smiling, then shaken his head and laughed. 'Jesus, how *was* that?'

Paul had smiled, too – although he'd also shrugged away from Simon's grip. Then he'd breathed in – tasted deep – tasted something like physics going quite awry, like unexpected possibility. 'It was all right.' He'd thought, for a second, the game might not be over.

'It was—' Simon had interrupted his outrage and checked Paul's face. 'Oh. Yeah.' He'd grinned. 'It was all right.' He'd seemed to consider for a moment. 'You feel a bit weird, yeah? Bit stunned? Mugged? Fuddled?'

To Paul, it hadn't felt quite appropriate that someone who was barely past teenage, who probably had at least one bad tattoo, and a no doubt exhaustive regimen of mildly unnerving self-abuse, was asking Paul about his personal condition.

Still, a response would do no harm, 'A little – a bit weird. Maybe. Yes. That stuff that he did with the ... the dead ...' It was sometimes good to make a conversation, join in.

'Then you should come along with me. You'll like this.' Simon had leaned in close enough to prove that his breath smelled of crisps. 'The show after the show.' But he'd also been unmistakably very serious and almost tender. 'Honest. It'll be good.' Simon had padded off without another glance, repeating as he went, 'How was that ... How just the bloody hell was that ... How was that ...' He'd expected Paul to follow.

And Paul had.

This isn't a chat-up, though, is it? Even if I was gay, he wouldn't be my taste at all – embarrassed if he'd think he was ...

Then again, he's clearly a nutter – so probably I'd fall for him completely.

Walking out of the theatre and round the bend.

Oh, quite exactly round the bend. And maybe here is where I get mugged. Factually, unmagically mugged. He'd be a really useless mugger, though – a lover, not a fighter: young Simon – well, a wanker, not a fighter. But he could have pals – mugger chums. Maybe.

Around one more corner and they'd stopped in a little lane.

This exact and precise little lane – this mildly cold and damp and faintly piss-and-disinfectant-scented lane – this lane at the back of the theatre where I am currently standing. After all this time. Still standing.

Worries had reeled by, but had left Paul curiously sanguine – unworried, in fact.

Still am – calm as you'd like.

Simon had brought him to see the stage door and the jovially restless cluster of other young men in black drainpipes, or disreputable coats, plus a scatter of slender, underdressed girls and a few motherly types.

'He'll be out in a while,' Simon had murmured as if he were in church. 'It's what he does. He comes and speaks to us.'

Paul had been mainly glad he didn't have to go home yet, but he couldn't help asking, 'What? Who does?'

'TGM. It's what he does. No photographs, no autographs – says then it isn't friendly – but he'll chat. To everyone. To you. Then it's like you're friends. We're his friends.'

'You're kidding.'

'Why would I be kidding?' Simon had frowned, but then was interrupted by the appearance of two stocky pals – real, non-mugger pals – in what Paul thought must be second-hand suits – or they possibly both enjoyed wearing their dads' clothes. While Paul watched, the three men had shaken hands and fussed in each other's pockets, producing a flurry of small trophies: wallets and house keys, bus passes and condoms and christknewwhat, which they had passed between themselves for a while, deadpan – stealing and passing, returning, then stealing again.

After reclaiming his unlikely handkerchief for the third time, Simon had nodded to indicate Paul. 'This is Paul. He gave me a ticket.'

'You want to watch that.' The more solemn newcomer had tugged at his walrus moustache and extended his arm. 'Hi. My name's Mr Palm.' He winked. 'You can call me Morritt.'

'And I would be Knot. Not Not – and not Knott – a K and one T – Knot. Davenport Knot – it's a family name.' The unmoustachioed Knot waved politely and inclined towards Simon. 'How many did you sneak in? Any? Were you trying? Did you get any? A few? You did try? Was there the offer of a finger ring at any point? A bit of badinage and word-age?' He'd nudged Paul lightly. 'Don't you just love words? Love-me things, lovely things.'

Simon had shrugged at Paul. 'They're feeling antisocial. So they're being ...'

'Playful.' Morritt had winked again. 'I'm always anti-social. Comes of being a sociopath.'

'Like I said, they're not in the mood for company, so I'll escort them and conduct what I will not at all or in any way describe as a debriefing over there.'

Morritt let his eyes grin but kept his face immobile and seemed to be searching Paul for something – not predatory, but curious, forensically interested.

'Morritt, leave him be.' Simon had patted Paul's shoulder. 'I'll be back in a bit. And—' He grinned like the boy he almost still was, 'Thanks again. Wouldn't have missed it.'

Which is how you end up standing by yourself and waiting. In a lane at night with your feet getting chilled – waiting for no one you'd wanted to meet in the company of strangers. And most of the strangers have headed off home.

All of the motherly women have gone, given up – except for the one with the shopping bag full of papers. Paul knew not to talk to her any more – and not to make eye contact, because that would start her off, as well.

'These are letters for TGM. I send them, but I know they don't get through. So I bring him the copies myself. He always smiles at me. He's lovely. He should eat more fruit.'

Paul had already been caught by her twice – once with the letter story and once with the much more complicated crap about there being some kind of grand conspiracy against magicians in general and TGM in particular – because he was so highly skilled – and only she knew how to stop it and TGM was fully aware of this and would one day ask her for her help which she would then graciously give. She was called Lucy.

Didn't want to know her name. Didn't want to know anything about her, or have anything to do with her. Funny, 'cos she's madder than anyone I've ever met and she does have nice tits. Big, anyway.

And she'd be grateful for the attention.

Sweet Jesus, what am I turning into.

And he glances at his watch to distract himself and it's ten past one and everybody's still here waiting – well, not so many as there were, but definitely some, a small crowd – eight people, counting himself, which he does, because he's people – and Paul has no way of being sure if this is normal – a three-hour wait. He doesn't like to interrupt Simon and his friends to ask them, because they seem to be enjoying themselves, giggling and showing each other cards, coins, little gadgets, and if he steps into that and messes it up for them, then he'll be the boring old bastard who knows nothing and shouldn't be here and he's sure that will make him depressed, so he won't attempt it and then he thinks that maybe the magician is busy and – here it comes as quick as fainting, weakness, shame – the sly, worst possible thought comes ramming in – he imagines that maybe Dee is here, maybe she came, maybe she'd talked about the magician because she knew him and maybe they're in there now, in his dressing room – lots of lights and a counter top, mirrors and maybe – why not – a bed – or a table – no, a bed – no, a hard, clinical table – and maybe he's touching her, maybe they're doing it, doing weird stuff, magician stuff, things that take three hours and counting, things that make her think the little bastard's really good, that open her and make her squeal it – he has this image of her skin and smears of make-up, stage make-up, of things that appear and disappear.

Except that's mad.

So mad it hurts.

Madder than Lucy.

I have no reasons to believe it, not one.

Stark, staring Lucy.

Mental.

As stupid as staying here when I ought to just chuck it and head for home.

But I've been here so long that I might as well keep on.

Paul's vaguely nauseous, though – images of clever fingers and slippery skin pitching in at him, so he walks a bit, strolls round, swallows and rubs his eyes, as if this will make the brain behind them sensible.

In a doorway, one of the three remaining girls is sitting and holding a programme and Paul thinks the step beneath her must be dirty and that's not right and she'll be perished and, to distract himself, he goes over and suggests, 'You could have my jacket. Borrow my jacket.'

She has dull blonde hair – 'No, it's okay' – and tiny wrists which manage to make Paul feel she has sometimes considered slashing them.

'You look freezing.' He wants to hold her, finds he is talking as if they have met before, are friends – the way you talk to people when you know how to talk to people.

'No, it's okay.'

She doesn't seem annoyed by him or anything, so he sits down next to her, is quiet for a bit, gives her time, and then, 'Do you like him – the magician?'

'Yeah.'

'And you want him to sign that. Your programme.'

She tucks her feet in nearer to herself, to the backs of her thighs. This will wrinkle her skirt. 'I don't think he's coming to see us tonight. It's late. He wouldn't make us hang around this long. Something must have happened. Guests. Or he's tired. Everyone else has come outside. Not him. He's gone another way.'

Paul sees how she is curled all to the left, beside the wall: trying to keep cosy, and thinks this must be uncomfortable and ineffective. Her blouse is old-fashioned, Laura Ashley, something like that – he can't really tell in the shadow.

'TGM doesn't sign things.' She yawns just enough to put a tremor in her jaw: a sweet, sweet trembling.

'No. I forgot.'

'What did you think?'

'About what?'

'The show.' This makes her begin to smile and he can imagine the same gentle, drowsy expression being there for some person who cares about her, lighting for them in a dawn with pillows and the spread of her hair. She faces him – perhaps studying, perhaps amused, he can't be sure – and asks again, 'What did you think? You haven't been before, have you? Whatever funny little club we are, you're not really in it yet.'

Paul wants to yawn, to join her in that – because yawns are infectious and he is tired and it would be very easy for him to tremble, 'I thought ...' Offer her a piece of himself that might seem sweet, and he would – by the way – like to see her hair on a pillow, anyone's hair on his pillow, 'I thought ...' But it's too late for that, doesn't matter, and it's fine for him to tell her now what's true – tell her as he would in a first morning when everything is interesting and you want to talk and you feel that you'll never get all that you need of this new woman and who she is and what she might enjoy and there is no pain from anywhere, not yet. 'I thought …' It's additionally fine – it will be absolutely fine, any disclosure – because in the morning this blonde whose name he does not know and will not ask will have forgotten him entirely. He'll be gone. 'I thought he was great.' All gone.

'But?'

'No but.' He smiles to reassure. 'Really. There's no but.' He knows he can hold her hand and she will not take it amiss, so he does, squeezes her fingers, cuddles them, and they sit together in the doorway with the cold of the stone underneath them and he says, 'I thought he was very good at what he does and … it was how he did it. Because of him not being that big, you know? He didn't look like a big man, not tall – and not, not some twat in a campy suit, or a Gandalf beard, or some kind of … I mean he's not a twat – and he was like my size – and ordinary, average – smart but average – and trying so hard to make these things happen, these bonkers things – and they did – he tried hard enough so that they did. I mean, it wasn't easy. Not that I didn't think he'd manage, just that it wasn't easy. He had to fight. It's all just fake, I get that – but he had to fight – he took the trouble to make it seem beyond him, impossible – and then he beat it. He won.'

Paul begins again with, 'For people like me ...' and then lets it fade. And he won't even attempt, 'And he was – he was like he was magnificent – because if you win you're allowed to be magnificent. You should be.' Because he thinks it would send him a little bit weepy – the way he'd got when there'd been that section in the second half: business that used a length of chain. He'd remember the chain: had a strong suspicion he would dream it, because it already had been half-turned to a dream when it was presented, there had been a quality about it that had slipped right in.

'When it lifted, when the chain lifted ... It's a trick, I know it's a trick – but it was right ... It was the way that you need it to be.'

She squeezes his fingers now. 'Like something coming true.'

It is pleasantly, slightly painful to consider this. 'Yeah.' The word seems damp and fluttery in his throat.

'That's what I come for.' And she pecks his cheek. 'That's why I come. To see that. Because it isn't real anywhere else.' And then she lets him go, because they are nothing to each other, he is nothing to her. 'I think I'll head home now.'

He is nothing to anyone. 'Will you be all right?' His knuckles feeling unnerved, stripped. He has the hands of no one.

'Yes.'

She stands, slightly unsteadily, and Paul rises with her and holds her shoulder for a breath. 'It was nice meeting you.'

'And it was nice meeting you.' This before she walks away, aiming for the street and a cab, he guesses. No other options beyond a cab at this time of night. Unless she's walking. Alone. Alone might not be safe.

Paul shouts after her, 'You'll be okay? Do you need somebody with you?' But she half-turns, waves her programme at him and shakes her head, keeps on round the corner and back to the usual, old world.

The other girls must have given up too, when he was occupied elsewhere, so there is Paul now and there is Lucy and Simon and his two companions with their imaginary names – each of them staring at Paul because he has called out. 'Sorry!' Although he isn't sorry. Quite the reverse.

Simon ambles over, 'No, I'm sorry. This is crazy. He's never this late. It's ... he never doesn't come out, but he never leaves it this late, so I don't know, mate. Don't think badly of him.'

'I don't.'

'Don't think badly of magic.'

'Oh, I don't.' Paul thinking of nothing but that chain: broad links, dull and heavy, dragged into the air, driven upwards by pure will and then compelled to disappear: a whole building of human beings casting them away and the magician there to hold their wish, find it, touch it out and show a proof of what they were and could be.

Just a trick. And just that last tangible moment before you're free – seeing that, for once seeing that. And if you can see it, then it can be and nothing left to hold you back. 'I don't think badly of it. Really. I had a good time. Thanks.'

Just a trick. But I could see it, see myself.

Now you see it.

Yes.

'You going home? It's past two.'

'Is it?' Paul's watch agreeing that suddenly it is past two and on the way to three. 'Oh. Might as well hang on a while longer, though – d'you think?'

Simon takes a pound coin and folds it into his hand and out and back and melts it somewhere between his fingers. 'Yeah, might as well.' He shrugs. 'Come and join us, guys.' He beckons his friends. 'The smug one's Barry and the miserable one's Gareth – his mum's Welsh.'

Gareth wanders towards them, avoiding Lucy, 'She wants to be Welsh. That's different.' And Barry follows, nodding.

The four of them slouch together in a huddle – they shift and cough.

'When he *does* come out …' Gareth tugs his moustache.

Barry reaches round and tugs it, too. 'You mean *if*.'

'When he *does* come out, we should all just ignore him –
like we're expecting someone else.'

They grin.

'No, but that would be rude, though.' Paul's sentence
fading as he starts to feel inept – spoiling the joke. 'I mean, if
we're his friends …' But then softly the men – Paul included –
begin to grin in the way that friends do, before they get to
trick their friends.

It's colder and the sky seems to rest down against them:
attentive, but wearying.

Paul understands the magician isn't coming. He also
understands it doesn't matter any more. They won't leave:
Simon, Barry, Gareth, Lucy – they'll stand here and he'll
stand with them – they're all going nowhere. Together.

*But that's fine, I'm just fine now. I know why I'm waiting for
him: The Great Man – I'm absolutely sure of that. I know exactly
what I'll ask him, what I need him to make me do.*

The Desert Torso

KAMILA SHAMSIE was born in 1973 in Karachi, Pakistan. She is the author of five novels: *In the City by the Sea, Salt and Saffron, Kartography, Broken Verses,* and most recently *Burnt Shadows* (2009), which has been shortlisted for the Orange Prize. She is also a reviewer and columnist, primarily for the *Guardian*

A MAN WALKS THROUGH the desert carrying a stone torso. It is all ribs and a swooping concaveness of stomach, a network of veins running web-like across the taut skin.

A day earlier, when the one who had travelled with it on the previous leg of its journey handed it over in the darkened interior of a bicycle repair shop, all that the man – Bilal – cared about was the weight of the torso. It was not as heavy as he had feared, but not as light as he had hoped for, either. The miles he would need to walk with it once the road ended and his brother's motorcycle could venture no further would only just be manageable.

Was it the weight of the thing which necessitated this multi-courier approach, he wondered? No single person had possession of it for more than a day, so the journey from Peshawar to the fringes of the Cholistan desert had already seen it pass through several sets of hands. But when the courier who preceded him handed it over to Bilal the former did not stretch and exhale in relief to be free of the stone; instead he seemed almost reluctant to part with it, and when he had finally helped Bilal strap it onto his back the other courier said, 'The longer you carry it, the lighter it gets.'

Bilal responded with a look that combined scepticism and disapproval. Such language was reserved for the meeting of the most sacred of relics and the most holy of men – such as the footprint of Hazrat Ali, embedded in a rock, which the Sufi Jahanian Jahangasht had carried on his back from Mecca to the town of Uch, which was just a few miles from this meeting place of the two couriers. When the great Sufi came upon the rock twenty men were trying, without success, to lift it. But to Jahanian Jahangasht – who performed Haj thirty-six times, with only his feet and camel to transport him – that rock weighed only one and a quarter kilograms.

'Don't forget,' the other courier said. 'Always keep it uncovered. If you try to hide it, people will know it's valuable. This way, you're just a crazy man carrying around a stone.' He walked out into the bright sunlight, pausing to pull a long stick of sugar-cane from the overladen donkey cart moving slowly along the road towards the cane threshers of the neighbouring village.

The crazy men were the foreigners, Bilal decided as he sat astride the motorbike, leaning against his brother's back so that the younger man, as he drove, could absorb some of the weight of the stone. Wasting all this money to have a stone transported halfway down and all the way across Pakistan from Peshawar to the Cholistan desert, from where it would enter India. What would happen to it once it got to India was something Bilal didn't much care about, though the man who had engaged him on this leg of the journey had said something about a museum far away as the stone's final destination.

Well, none of it mattered to Bilal except the cash he'd received in advance and the cash he'd receive on completion. In the last few years as visa regulations between India and Pakistan had relaxed it had become harder to find people so desperate to cross the border to see family on the other side that they'd pay for this desert route through no-man's land. Though – thank god for blood-soaked mercies – after the recent Bombay carnage the visa flow had slowed to a trickle, and soon business would pick up again. But so would the landmines along the unpatrolled border. The nomad he paid to keep him informed of such activity assured him that so far there had been no re-mining and his old maps would still see him safely across, but since the time of the Kargil crisis when he'd seen a camel and its rider burst into guts and flesh just fifty paces ahead of him in the sand, he'd known that even the nomads couldn't always keep up with the mining activities of both India and Pakistan's armies.

Regardless of border tensions, the stone was less trouble to transport than a human, plus he'd been able to charge double his normal amount for it. He rested his cheek on his brother's back, watching mustard fields fly past – yellows and greens so bright they could make your eyes hurt – on the irrigated side of the road. The other side was desert and scrub.

Perhaps it would be worthwhile to look more seriously into becoming a courier of relics. The Taliban's influence was only going to spread, and there had to be many more such idols in Pakistan, and also many stoneworkers who could be paid a small amount to replicate them by the dozen. He fell asleep against his brother's back, smiling to think of this new business venture.

When he woke up, a woman was pressed against him.

It took a moment to realise there was only stone at his back. But what a moment that was.

When the motorcycle skidded to a stop at the end of the track, his brother untied the stone from Bilal's back and for the first time Bilal paused to examine the thing. What kind of people revere a figure so horribly emaciated, was his first thought. It was something he'd never understood about other religions – how they turned images of suffering into objects of worship. As children he and his brother had once entered a church at night, through a broken window, and when Bilal had switched on the torch the beam swung across the little room and found a hand with a nail driven through the palm. He had dropped the torch in terror, and as it fell from his grasp it illuminated ribs, blood, nailed feet before mercifully shattering on the church floor. He had scrambled out of the broken window so fast he cut his own hands and feet on the jagged pane.

Years later, he felt something of the same terror as his brother ran his fingers along the net of veins that criss-crossed the stone torso.

'Don't,' he said and, against instruction, draped his shawl over the torso before tucking it firmly under his arm.

In films the desert sands were always golden, and the desert was made for men's desires – all swells and dips, one curve leading to the next. But here the land was flat and brown, thorny bushes breaking up the vista. The nomads swore you could still find shells dating back to the time when the Hakra River flowed through here, when their people had settled abodes and didn't have to spread through Asia and Europe learning to treat mobility as the state in which they felt most at home. The Hakra had dried up centuries and centuries before the stone beneath his arm was carved into rib and vein, even though it was nearly two thousand years ago that this stone was stone and not just a breath away from breath.

Where had that thought come from?

He brought one end of his shawl over his head to protect it from the maddening influence of the sun. The other end continued to keep the unbreathing stone hidden from all eyes.

How he hated the desert! He placed one foot in front of the next, feeling the give of sand beneath his shoes. An hour of walking on such yielding ground with this thing nestled beneath his arm and he knew he'd start yearning for a camel. But the rising prices, the declining border crossings over the previous year, had left him deeply in debt; he couldn't afford to hire a boy to carry the stone for him, let alone a camel.

Fifteen years ago he wouldn't have believed anyone who told him he'd come to hate the desert. He first came here as a schoolboy, with an older cousin, who took him to the Derawar Fort with its forty ramparts and told him about Alexander's treasure, which still remained hidden somewhere on the premises, despite all the attempts to find it. He had believed that, like the footprint of Hazrat Ali, the treasure required a specific person to lift it out and carry it away – and why shouldn't he be that person? He even brushed aside the chance to join in a game of cricket in the forecourt of the fort complex, using an old cannon as the wicket, in favour of wandering through each crumbling room, each bat- and rat-infested cellar and dungeon, in the

hope the treasure would recognise him and reveal itself.
Later that day, his father had hit him – how dare he compare
the treasure of a pagan to the footprint of Hazrat Ali? Bilal
knew he should keep quiet but he couldn't stop himself
from repeating what he had earlier heard: Alexander – the
great Sikandar – was mentioned in the Quran and Hazrat
Ali was not.

That was the day he had the sacredness of the sacred
beaten into him, not just skin deep, but deeper than that –
as deep as cuts and bruises, deep as terror.

The thing beneath his arm grew heavier. He shifted it to
the other arm.

By the time he reached the ancient, crumbling structure
in which he was to stop for the night, both arms burned
with soreness. He had never been so happy to see his resting place before, not even that time when the family he
was transporting had all become sun-struck to the point of
near delirium and he'd had to slap and kick them to keep
them moving.

The roof had gone, and the stone walls of the one-room
structure had half-collapsed over the centuries – or was it
merely years? He had no way of knowing how long ago the
foundations had been laid – but even so, there was some
protection against the cold night air. He laid the torso on
the ground and then, groaning with the effort of it, pushed

aside the rubble at one end of the room which looked to the unknowing eye as though it were nothing but a collapsed wall rather than a carefully constructed hiding place, and pulled out the blankets, oil lantern and ropes of onion that were buried in a shallow hole in the sand beneath.

The light of the lantern, when he set it down, fell directly on the torso. He squatted next to it and rested his hand on the stone, the heel of his palm on the cage of ribs, the fingers touching the four folds of flesh right above the belly button which attested to a former sleekness. He picked up a stone from the scattered rubble, about the same size as the torso, and placed it beside the torso. Then he raised his kameez and looked down at his own stomach. There was loose skin, forming two neat folds, above his own belly button. Business had been very bad, food prices astronomical.

He looked from stone to stone torso to his own torso for a few seconds, then hurriedly – in the manner of a man shaking himself from a trance – lowered his kameez and turned his back on the torso, searching among the rubble for the smoothest stone.

Once found, the smooth stone became his pillow. He covered himself with the blankets and spread the ropes of onion around his sleeping area to ward off snakes before blowing out the lantern flame. Usually after this walk he'd be asleep in seconds, but today he was awake long enough to see all the stars come out, and the moon rise until it was right above the structure.

How thrilling it had been when he was a child – the news that Alexander was mentioned in the Quran. It made him part of Islamic history, made him someone Bilal could claim. In history classes in school there was always this lingering sense of loss when the teacher talked about Pakistan's history before 1947 – it seemed most of the most important locations of the history of Muslims in the subcontinent had stayed in India: Agra, Delhi, Panipat. But when he told his history teacher about Alexander and the Quran, the old man said that was only one interpretation of the verse in question, and he was personally not inclined to believe that the reference was to Alexander. And so Alexander shifted back into that grey area – along with the Indus Valley Civilisation, and stones such as the one now lying just feet away from him – where the history of the nation of Pakistan and the history of the territory that constituted Pakistan separated.

A cloud passed over the moon; the light falling around Bilal wavered; he thought he saw the torso move. He closed his eyes and recited Ayat-ul-Kursi until the world became dreamlike.

Afterwards, he would always struggle to remember the noise which awoke him. It wasn't a hissing, or a slithering across sand – of that he was sure. But his eyes opened to the sight of a snake twisting sideways along the stone torso. He had never seen the breath-drinking snake of the desert – but he'd heard from the nomads that it crawled onto men's chests and poisoned their breath. He sat up slowly. The snake raised its head, and he wondered if it was confused to find a chest with no head attached. But then it lowered its head, its tongue flickering out into the space between one fragile rib and the next ...

And somehow Bilal found himself swinging the lantern, his movements so measured that the base of the lantern clipped the snake's body and lifted it off the torso with enough momentum to send it flying through the air. When it landed, just outside the stone structure, it disappeared into the sand and darkness.

The sound of heartbeats was so loud it couldn't be Bilal's heart alone. He lay down and drew the torso close to him, draping one onion-rope over the chest like a garland, his fingers gently prodding the space between ribs where the snake's tongue had flickered. His finger came away moist. Whispering apologies, he bent his head towards the ancient chest and kissed away what venom remained.

When he rested his head on the chest, he felt those veins, those ribs pressing against his cheek, the slow thud of a heart beneath.

He understood them now, the ones who would destroy such things. They knew, as he never had, how these figures could inspire worshipfulness. They knew that to look too long at even a fold of skin above the figure's belly button might make them pause in the midst of battle to search among rubble for a stone with a beating heart.

They were right to be terrified. They were right to think their world would be safer it if were destroyed. Life could be controlled so long as this was destroyed. Stone could return to being stone, cargo transported across the border could be cargo once more. A man could ignore every heartbeat, even his own. The ones who wanted to destroy the figure understood all this; perhaps the ones who wanted to encase it in glass away from searching fingers and worshipping mouths understood it, too.

In the morning he felt refreshed. The stiff neck he always woke with after a night on a stone pillow was entirely absent after his many hours of resting against the hollow stomach of his travelling companion.

He lifted him gently off the sand, cradling him. The world had never been so clear before, the desert never so beautiful. He would walk through the desert with this life in his arms. He would walk until he could walk no more, and when he stopped the desert sands would cover him, and they would cover the Buddha, and one of them would die, and one of them would wait until the world was ready to uncover him.

Goodnight Children,
Everywhere

BERYL BAINBRIDGE was born in Liverpool in 1934. She has written eighteen novels, five of which have been Booker-nominated. *Every Man for Himself* won the Whitbread Novel Award and *Master Georgie* won the James Tait Black Memorial Prize and the WH Smith Literary Award. Her most recent novel, *According to Queeney* (2001), is the story of Dr Johnson's relationship with Hester Thrale. She was made a DBE in 2001.

THOMAS WAS ELEVEN YEARS OLD and had no brothers or sisters. Or a father, for that matter. This didn't worry him. Except Ringo, his bestest friend, none of the boys in his class had one, and his dad often came home drunk.

Thomas's mother had a full-time job as a typist in an estate agent's; recently she had become very anxious because there was a slump in house buying and she feared being made redundant, whatever that was. She'd started smoking again. Mostly Thomas was in the care of Mildred, his grandmother. She was pretty old, bad at climbing stairs and always mislaying her teeth. She also talked a lot about God, who had mostly let her down. When he was seven and had asked his mother what this meant, he was ordered to mind his own business. Aged ten and putting forward the same question, he was told she'd been handed a cruel slice of life, that hers had not been a happy journey. After a lot of probing he learned that his grandfather had been a violent man, that he had punched his wife so brutally that she'd ended up in a hospital bed.

'Did he punch you too?' asked Thomas, feeling hot all over, but Mother said he'd gone away a month before she was born.

Often Mildred referred to him as 'Ginger Tom', which annoyed him, though not deeply; he did have red hair. His mum said he must never be rude to Mildred, however aggravating, because of the past, which was odd seeing she often told Mildred to shut up.

He and Mum lived near the Bottle Factory, on the third floor of a block of flats, which was why Thomas went to Mildred's house every day after school and stayed there until his mother fetched him. His grandmother's legs were as unreliable as the dicky lift provided by the flats. Sometimes his friend Ringo would ask him to come home with him, but mostly he refused, saying his grandmother needed him. Once Bernadette Mills, who had dyed yellow streaks in her hair, invited him to tea at her house, but Ringo warned him off; Bernadette was into kissing, which was boring unless a puppy was involved.

He was happy at school, particularly when taught by Mrs Vosper, the religious studies teacher, who was always talking about inner voices. Outside of us all, she insisted, is the apparent world, but inside lies the real truth trying to break through. They should listen. Ringo declared she was potty, and when Thomas told his mother what Mrs Vosper had said she shouted it was bloody ridiculous that her hard-earned earnings were being taxed to provide a livelihood for a mad woman. Being Mother, she'd got over it by morning.

The nice thing for Thomas was the amount of old-fashioned stuff which his grandmother Mildred kept stored in the second bedroom. There was a gramophone that would only work if wound up with a handle, a brass samovar that heated water if you lit a candle under it, and an army box containing a steel helmet full of toy soldiers, a dozen gold bullets and a jack-in-the-box that played a tune when you thumped the button and Jack shot up. Best of all was the ancient radio – Mildred called it a wireless – encased in mahogany. She'd inherited it from her mother, and said it was broken – something to do with the air waves not being able to get through any more. She didn't like him talking about it and refused to let him bring it downstairs; not that he could have, it being so heavy.

The first time Thomas stuck its plug into the mains he just heard a crackling sound, like people walking across melting snow. He fiddled with the switches for an hour or more and heard nothing beyond the crackles and was just about to give up when a voice, very posh, very serious, announced that a man called Ramsay MacDonald had just died. Thomas took in the name on account of it being the same as that of his science teacher, a shy man who struggled to keep order in class; he rode a bike and had a small lump at the side of his right eye, which he constantly touched when the noise got too loud and he grew flustered. When Thomas went to school the next day he intended to ask if the dead man was a relation, but Ringo urged him against it in case the bigger lads accused him of trying to become teacher's pet.

Mildred didn't believe him when he said the radio worked. 'And when it's over,' he said, 'a man says "Goodnight children, everywhere".' Mildred was cooking him fish fingers for his tea and shook the pan so hard that the fat spat onto her arm. She said she was going to get Mr Eccles next door to carry the wireless down to the bins. Fortunately she forgot about it.

After that first time Thomas listened to the wireless every night while waiting for Mother to collect him. There was always something of interest, though when he repeated any of it to Mildred she seemed confused. For instance, when he told her that somewhere in America a wall had crashed down and that lots of people were throwing themselves out of windows, she looked puzzled. Even more so when he gave her the news that Mr Baldwin had just agreed to build up the Air Force. 'Mr Baldwin?' she repeated. 'Can't be … you misheard.'

On the Wednesday he listened to a broadcast to do with the disappearance on board a ship of a man called Frank Vosper. The name was familiar. During an early morning party on board, in the company of a well-known beauty queen and another guest, Mr Vosper had wandered off to take some air at a window. Despite an intensive search by crew and passengers, as well as the use of a dog belonging to a blind man, he couldn't be found. When the ship docked at Plymouth and the news was broken to his family, his father had a heart attack and died. It was decided not to bury him until his son's body was found.

A week later, at morning assembly, the headmaster said he had some sad news to impart, concerning Mrs Vosper, the religious studies teacher. She would be absent for some days owing to hearing that morning of a tragic accident which last night had resulted in the death of her brother. A minute's silence was requested. Thomas stood very still, head bowed.

That evening when Thomas switched on the wireless he heard of three other deaths which had taken place that day, followed by an account of what the deceased had done in life. Twice it was a person he'd heard of, a man called James Barrie who had written a famous pantomime and then a

John D. Rockefeller who was very rich and had given his money away to the poor. The third death was of a woman who'd been stabbed in Tesco's in full view of other customers. She hadn't done anything in life – at least, nothing that needed to be told.

Thomas was bothered about Mr Barrie because when he was little his grandmother had taken him to see *Peter Pan* and he remembered her telling him that Mr Barrie had died before the war. She said it was the same year that Neville Chamberlain had complained of England not spending enough on armaments. When he mentioned Mr Rockefeller's name to his mother, she remarked that it was a pity he'd gone because he might have been able to help with the credit crunch. Thomas didn't know what that meant; it sounded like a chocolate bar.

When he came home from school the next day there were police outside the flats. His grandmother was crying. She'd just got back from shopping when she'd seen a neighbour attacked with a knife; she was dead, lying just below a shelf of pork pies.

After some thought Thomas decided to confide in Mr MacDonald. He didn't let on to Ringo and waited until the big boys had gone home. He found the teacher in the bicycle shed, bending down to adjust his trouser clips.

'My radio', Thomas said, 'is acting funny.'

'In what way?' asked Mr MacDonald.

Thomas said it crackled a lot. He couldn't think of the words he really wanted.

'I can't be of much help', Mr MacDonald said, 'without looking at its interior.'

Greatly daring, Thomas asked if he could spare the time to come home with him, his grandmother's house being only round the corner. Mr MacDonald said he'd come willingly, if he was sure Thomas's family wouldn't think it an intrusion. He refused to step into the house until Mildred hobbled into the hall and said he was welcome.

Mr MacDonald was equally enthusiastic about the old radio. He went so far as to call it a work of art. He remembered his uncle having one almost like it, though not so shiny. When he turned the knob, no voice came on, just the crackling. He listened to this and said it could be mended but it would be expensive to replace the electronic tubes.

'But it works already,' Thomas insisted. 'This morning it mentioned that this month twelve hundred and forty-seven people died in a flu epidemic.'

Mr MacDonald stared at him.

'Then it talked about a man called Oswald Mosley, who was unconscious because he'd had a brick thrown at him in Liverpool.'

'Mosley?' questioned Mr MacDonald.

'Oswald,' said Thomas. 'He's some kind of agitator. It was about half an hour after Uncle Mac came on to say, "Goodnight children, everywhere".'

Mr MacDonald continued to stare; there was a hint of alarm in his eyes. Thinking it was the type of news, the dwelling on death, that was worrying his teacher, Thomas mentioned that a lot of things he listened to were about religion and the love of God. This wasn't the exact truth, though there had been a talk a week ago about Christ on the Cross and how he had trembled when the nails were banged in.

Mr MacDonald went home soon after. Mildred offered to make him a cup of tea. He refused, on the grounds that he was off to a wrestling class.

'Why?' she asked.

'Something to take up the time,' he replied, stroking the skin beside his eye. At the door he paused and suggested to Mildred that it might be a good idea to get Thomas's mother to encourage him to read a bit more, rather than fiddle with the radio. Thomas heard him but wasn't worried; Mildred had a memory like a sieve.

The next morning, at school, Mr MacDonald asked him to come to the staff room in the lunch hour. It meant Thomas had to cancel going to the chip shop with Ringo.

'I've brought you here,' began Mr MacDonald, 'because I'm impressed at your interest in history. Your interpretation of the past is far beyond your years. The first and foremost step in all knowledge of mankind is the conviction that a man's conduct, in all essential particulars, is governed not by reason but by his innate and unalterable character.'

Thomas smiled; he hadn't understood a word.

'Wisdom,' Mr MacDonald continued, 'which is only theoretical and never put into practice, is like a double rose: its colour and perfume delightful, but ... but ...' here he hesitated as if searching his mind, '... one must realise that history, in its dictionary definition, deals with events only in the past. You understand what I'm saying?'

Thomas said, 'Of course.' He felt sorry for Mr MacDonald.

That night when he switched on the radio it was announced that a queen had died, widow of Edward VII. It was said she had lived amongst vases filled with roses. There followed an alarming account of an explosion to do with faulty gas pipes at a school, causing the death of a teacher and twenty-four pupils.

The next morning Thomas clutched his stomach and stayed in bed. 'I'm not well,' he wailed, and added, though his mother didn't hear, 'I want to live.'

The newspapers published a story to do with the school explosion, mentioning that the dead teacher, a Mr MacDonald, had been in an agitated state at assembly that day. Several times he had shouted out, 'It's Children's Hour.'

Later, Thomas smashed up the radio with a hammer.

The Night Highway

LOUISE WELSH studied history at Glasgow University, then for several years ran a second-hand bookshop. Her first novel, *The Cutting Room*, won several awards, including the 2002 Crime Writers' Association John Creasey Memorial Dagger. It was followed by *Tamburlaine Must Die* (2004), a novelette written around the final three days of the poet Christopher Marlowe's life. Her latest novel is *The Bullet Trick* (2006), set in Berlin and Glasgow, about a down-at-heel conjuror. 'The Night Highway' is a work in progress from a new novel.

MURRAY'S TINY OFFICE was almost but not quite dark. Enough light shone in from the streetlamp beyond the trees for him to see Rachel Houghton's face twist towards the expression he was striving for. A blast of hail shot against the window and Rachel's pupils widened, edging nearer, but still too self-aware to be there yet. Murray matched his rhythm to the shadows cutting across the room – God, it had turned into a filthy night – blessing whatever procurer of office furniture had managed to issue him with a desk of exactly the right height. Rachel's heels spurred him on. He could feel the soft leather of her shoes, the spike of their stilettos.

'No,' he said, 'don't or ...'

Her ankles gripped him tighter. Murray felt a draught touch his exposed rear and a thin slice of light cut into the room illuminating Rachel's face, her eyes slitting against the sudden brightness, looking beyond him to the opening door. Murray half cursed, half groaned as he leaned into her, his arse bared to the intruder and that final look of pleasure still not won.

Murray extricated himself and stumbled into the hallway, almost catching the door before it closed. He shouted something, as he ran, some bark of protest, his unfastened shirt flapping open, the air of the darkened corridor cold against his chest. But whoever it was had vanished, lost in the gloomy hallways that made up the old buildings. The only comfort was he'd remembered to hold on to his trousers instead of letting them ambush him by the ankles and send him sprawling, like the comedy lover he so obviously was.

'I've no idea who it was. Probably a porter doing his rounds.' Rachel stepped behind the desk and began to pull on her abandoned tights. 'More frightened of us than we were of him.'

A few years ago they would have had the surety of a cigarette to smooth the post-coital awkwardness. But these days smoking in university buildings was grounds for dismissal. Fortunately fucking didn't set off the sprinkler system. Murray fumbled his belt buckle into place and sank into the chair usually designated for visiting students. He lifted a first-year essay that only seconds ago had rustled beneath

Rachel's bottom and tried to smooth out the creases in its paper.

… *he succeeded against the odds. Though his lifestyle was deemed unacceptable by mainstream society his …*

The page bounced stubbornly back. Murray replaced it on the desk, weighting the bent corner with a mug. A little cold coffee slopped onto the neatly printed words.

'Fuck.' He blotted the stain with the front page of the *Guardian*. 'Was he wearing a porter's uniform?' Murray peeled the newspaper back. A dark shadow of newsprint remained, stamped across the dutifully prepared argument. 'Shit.'

'I told you, I didn't get a good look at him. It was dark and I was … slightly distracted.'

Murray wondered if he should have carried on chasing the intruder. He had been breathing in the distinctive reek of recalcitrant students, frustrated scholars and books since he was a seventeen-year-old undergraduate. These corridors' twists and turns were mapped on his mind. He knew all the cubbyholes and suicide steps. The lecture halls racked with seating, the illogical staircases that tricked the uninitiated but led eventually to the out-of-bounds attics from where a man could lose himself and emerge on the opposite side of the old campus. The chances of catching whoever it was were radically slimmer than the odds of looking like an out-of-breath idiot. But the part of him that imagined grabbing the peeping Tom's collar and administering his boot to the seat of their breeks wished he'd given it a shot.

Rachel tugged the hem of her skirt down. Usually she wore trousers. She had, he realised, very good legs.

'You look nice.'

Rachel flashed him the same bright smile that she gave to shop assistants, students, fellow lecturers, porters, her husband, anyone who crossed her path when her mind was elsewhere. He watched as she took a small mirror from her handbag. Her lipstick was hardly smudged, but she perched on the edge of his desk and reapplied it anyway. Murray was reminded of an early portrait of Christie by the lover who had preceded Archie. It had been painted before she escaped to Edinburgh. She must have been barely seventeen, but in the painting she was ageless, long legs, sharp angles and red lips. It was a good look.

The memory of the opening door, the light shifting across Rachel's face, returned, spoiling the knowledge that she'd dressed up for him. He measured the trajectory between their clinch and the door with his thumb and forefinger.

'You don't think it was someone from the department?'

Rachel's smile grew tight. She dropped the mirror back into her bag and zipped it shut.

'It's Friday evening. No one else would be in their office at this time. Most of them have something that passes for a life. Don't worry. We probably made his night. No doubt he's crouched in the gatehouse right now, reliving the memory.'

'Of my white arse? I bloody hope not.'

'Irresistible. Your white arse will have a starring role in that little bit of ciné film that plays behind his eyes when he goes home and rogers his tired, but pleasantly surprised, old wife for the first time in months.'

Rachel was on his side of the desk now. Her skirt was made of some kind of shiny, silver-grey fabric, stretched taut across her hips. Murray ran a finger down her leg, feeling the satin slide of the material. She placed a hand on his, stopping its progress, and he leaned back in his chair.

'So what's the occasion?' He wanted to keep her there a while, or maybe be with her somewhere else. Somewhere with subdued lighting, candles, soft music – what a cliché. It was Friday night and most people had a life. 'Fergus taking you somewhere nice?'

'Fergus doesn't take me places. We go together.'

Murray put his foot against the desk and leaned back in his chair. If he were a cowboy he'd have tipped his hat forward. She hadn't dressed for him, after all. He tried for playful and failed. 'We could go together better.'

Rachel bent towards him. He felt her breath, warm and sweet, with a faint scent of peppermint. She'd started smoking again.

'One of the things I've always appreciated about Fergus is that he's never boring.'

'He bored me rigid at the last faculty meeting.' Murray reached into his desk drawer and fished out the bottle of malt he'd bought weeks ago in the hope of tempting her to stay longer than the time it took to straighten her clothes. 'I think I need a drink. Do you want to join me?' He hesitated. 'Or we could go somewhere, if you'd prefer a glass of wine.'

Rachel glanced at the clock above the office door. Murray wondered if she'd been keeping an eye on the time during their lovemaking.

'I told you. I can't stay long. We're having people round for dinner. Fergus is making his famous shepherd's pie.'

'Proletarian heartiness the latest smart thing?'

'I hope so. It's certainly more economical than some of Fergus's enthusiasms. Here,' she reached into her bag and drew out a bottle of Blackwood's, 'I'll have a splash of this. My alibi.'

Alibi. The word irritated him.

'How long will it excuse you for?'

'Long enough. Fergus was determined to have Shetland gin for aperitifs. They don't sell it everywhere. Why?' She had a pointed face, like a sly little fox. Sometimes when she smiled she looked a short leap away from a bite. 'Are you scared he might hunt me down?'

Murray got up and washed his coffee cup. The light stretching across the room was snagged in his mind. Fergus was at least fifteen years older than Rachel, somewhere in his fifties, but he'd run the 10k last year. Could he have covered the stretch of the corridor in the time it had taken Murray to get to the door? But why would Fergus run? He had the power to fell Murray without lifting a fist. He ignored Rachel's question, taking the gin from her and pouring a little into the clean mug.

'Sorry about the crockery – not very suave.'

'Not being very suave is part of your charm.'

'Then you won't be surprised to hear I can't offer you ice and lemon.'

'A little water will be fine.'

It was part of what he'd liked about her, this posh gameness. In another era she would have made a great lady explorer. He could imagine her cajoling a team of native carriers through the jungle, taking one of them to her tent at night, then ordering him to pick up and carry her bundles the next morning.

He went to the sink. Usually he drank the bottled stuff, convinced he could taste the liquorice taint of lead in the university tap water, but there was only a small dreg left in the plastic bottle of Strathmore in his rucksack. He let the cold run for a moment, then added a dash to her cup.

'Thanks.'

Rachel smiled, holding it against her chest while he poured himself a nip of the whisky. He was going to clink his cup against hers, but she took a sip of the gin grimacing, then coughing against its burn.

Murray laughed.

'A hardy people, these Shetlanders.' He tasted his own drink and considered coughing for comedy value, but didn't. He'd played the fool enough for one night. 'Doesn't it bother you? Our visitor?'

'You shielded me.'

He toasted her with his mug.

'Instinctive chivalry.'

'Of course it bothers me.' She glanced at the clock again. 'But it's happened. What's the point in torturing ourselves? A rumour will start or a rumour won't start. We'll worry about it if it does. The thing we have to make sure of is that it doesn't happen again.'

'You're right. It was stupid, doing it here.'

'That wasn't what I meant.' She saw the expression on his face and smiled. 'We both know it can't go on.'

He couldn't trust his voice. He hadn't known, didn't know.

'And you're going to be on sabbatical for a year.' She brightened, like a children's nurse who had applied Dettol to a skinned knee and was now about to use a sweet to distract attention from the sting. 'You won't have time for all this.'

He tried to keep his words light.

'There's only so much time you can spend on research. I'm sure I could have squeezed you in.'

'We agreed it would only ever be a bit of fun. Anyway term's almost over. Fergus and I are going to Umbria for two months, and you're starting your sabbatical. It makes sense.'

'If we hadn't been interrupted?'

'What does it matter?' She leaned forward and kissed him gently on the mouth for the last time. 'We had fun. We like each other. Let's keep it that way.'

His voice was steady. He'd read about well-integrated autistics, they had to think about every gesture, *smile, make eye contact*. He formed his mouth into a grin.

'You're right. It was fun while it lasted.'

Rachel touched his arm.

Don't flinch, don't argue, don't push her away.

'It'll be a great book. You're always saying how underrated Lunan is. This is your big chance to put him on the map.'

'I hope so.'

'I know so. Fergus does too.'

The pair of them discussing him. Where? Over dinner? In bed? Did he ever feature in the little bit of ciné film she ran behind her eyes while Fergus fucked her?

He said, 'Rachel, Fergus can't stand me.'

She took her coat from the hook on the back of the office door.

'Don't be so paranoid, Murray. You know Fergus: if he didn't think you were a valuable member of the department you wouldn't be enjoying a year's sabbatical; you'd be look-ing for a new post.'

Murray stood at his office window. It was still wild outside. The wind caught at Rachel's hair, blowing it across her face. She struggled for a moment with the car door, then she was in, headlamps on, reversed out and away, her only backwards glance at the road behind through the rear-view mirror. It was the last time, the open door, his invitation. He stood at the window for a couple of minutes, watching the trees fingering the sky the same way they would if he weren't there. On his way out he stopped by the gatehouse and handed the almost full bottle of malt to the porter, who received it with grateful, bland surprise.

The reasons Murray Watson usually avoided Fowlers were clustered around their customary corner table, looking like a eugenicist's nightmare. The pub wasn't busy, but it was warming up with the overspill of office workers and students from more popular establishments, so he was halfway to the bar before he spotted Ray Costello, Lyle Joff and Phylida McWilliams and remembered that this was where they congregated late on Friday afternoons, playing at being the Algonquin club and staving off the wretchedness of the weekend.

Maybe the need to suffer that misery so often brings in its wake would have led him into their company anyway, or maybe he would have settled for a lone pint and a nod in their direction, but then he felt a hand on his elbow and turned to see Rab Purvis's face, shiny with sweat and bonhomie.

'I'll get this, Moira.' It was typical of Rab to be on first-name terms with the manageress, typical too of him to add Murray's drink to the round and a tip on top of the price. Mrs Noon nodded her thanks and Rab gave Murray's elbow a squeeze that told him his friend was at least three pints to the good. 'Come away into the body of the kirk.'

It had drifted beyond the time when even late diners could pretend to be having a pre-prandial, and the department's dwindling stock of alcoholics welcomed Murray with hearty relief. He was the fresh blood, the bringer of new topics, the excuse to get another round in and postpone the moment when the pub door swung home and they each stepped out alone.

'Hello stranger.' Phylida McWilliams's voice had lost its usual edge and now held the full throaty promise of a pack of unfiltered Camels. She leaned over and gave Murray a kiss. 'Why do we never see you?'

Murray didn't bother to mention that she'd passed him in the corridor three days ago, her head bowed, looking like Miss Marple's hungover younger sister.

'You know how it is, Phylida. I'm a busy little bee.'

Phylida picked a blonde hair from Murray's lapel and raised her eyebrows.

'He's a "B" alright,' said Ray Costello. 'Leave him alone, Phyl. You don't know where he's been.'

The woman let the hair fall from her fingers onto the barroom floor. She nodded. 'Many a true word.'

'He flits from flower to flower.'

Rab conducted a little minuet in the air with his hand and Phylida laughed her barmaid's laugh.

'Where the bee sucks so suck I.'

It was worse than he'd thought. They must have been there for hours. Murray wondered if they suspected about Rachel. He should go home, make himself something to eat, think things through.

Lyle Joff began an anecdote about a conference he'd attended in Toronto. Phylida clamped an interested expression onto her face and Ray Costello rolled the beer around in his glass, staring sadly into space. Over by the bar Mrs Noon turned up the music and Willie Nelson started to serenade the Whisky River, begging it never to run dry and to take care of him for as long as it flowed.

Murray laughed and shook his head. 'Pure poetry.'

'I can't bear this over-elevation of popular culture. It's a catchy tune, nothing more.' Rab had never learned the difference between the modulations required in the lecture hall and in those suitable to social situations. A couple of recently arrived drinkers glanced over, but Rab's harmless old duffer disguise rendered him safe as a madman in Apache country. 'John Donne writes poetry, W.H. Auden writes poetry, Philip Larkin writes poetry. There are some who even allege that Andrew Motion writes poetry, but this chap,' Rab cocked his ear theatrically as if weighing up the merits of the music, 'this chap composes foot-tapping numbers.'

'It speaks to me, Rab.' Murray put his hand in the centre of his chest. 'It touches my heart.' He knocked back the last of his pint. 'What's everyone drinking?'

Ray Costello broke out of his trance. He necked the last three inches of his beer.

'It's my shout.'

He placed his hand on top of Phylida McWilliams's and she let him keep it there for a moment before drawing hers away.

Murray wondered if Ray's divorce was finalised and if he had moved out of the family home yet, or if he was still camping in the space that had once been his study.

'Not for me, thanks.' Joff tipped his glass to his lips and the last of his heavy slid smoothly down. 'It's past my curfew.' He gave Murray a complicit look. 'Bedtime story duty, *Winnie the Pooh*, a marvellous antidote to a hard day at the coalface.'

As preposterous as the image of chubby Joff at a coalface was, it seemed more feasible than the picture of him sitting at the bedside of freshly washed, pyjama-clad toddlers, reading about talking bears and excited tigers. Murray had been introduced to Lyle's wife at a faculty party once; she was prettier than he'd expected. He wondered how they'd met and why Joff was so often in the early evening company of people for whom the only alternative to the pub was the empty flat, the armchair tortured with cigarette burns and the book collection that was only so much comfort.

Ray Costello looked at his watch.

'It's gone half nine. They'll be safe in the land of Nod by now surely, long past breathing in your boozy breath, Lyle.'

Joff looked at his own watch as if astonished to see that the hands had moved round. He hesitated, then looked at his glass as if equally amazed to find it empty.

'You'll get me shot, Costello.' He grinned. 'Just one more for the road, then.'

Ray raised his empty glass in the air until he caught the attention of Mrs Noon. He held five fingers up and the manageress gave a curt dip of her head to show she'd oblige, but only for the moment.

Phylida leaned over and whispered, 'You're a cunt, Ray. You won't be happy until that boy's marriage has gone the same way as yours and you've got a full-time drinking companion.'

'Why would I need that when I've got you, Phyl?'

Costello gave her a hug. Phylida pushed him away.

'You forget yourself sometimes.'

Drink took the sting from the scold but there was a seed of bitterness in the mellow voice that would blossom with more watering, and when Ray tried for a second squeeze her shove was impatient.

The tray of drinks arrived and Lyle Joff helped himself to a fresh pint. He took a sip and wiped the foam from his top lip.

'There's nothing wrong with my marriage.'

'I'm sure it's rock solid.' Rab patted Lyle's arm and asked Murray, 'Have you met Lyle's wife? A beautiful girl, classical profile, a touch of the Venus de Milo about her.'

He winked and Murray wearily took his cue.

'Armless?'

'Wouldn't hurt a fly.'

Phylida laughed and Lyle said, 'Built on strong foundations. Love, affection, shared values.'

He looked into the middle distance as if trying to recall other reasons his marriage would endure.

'Children,' Phylida said. 'Children are a blessing.' And Ray Costello excused himself to go to the Gents.

'That'll be the last we see of him tonight,' whispered Rab, angling his chair towards Murray, separating him from the rest of the company. But Costello was back soon enough, adjusting his flies as he crossed the barroom floor.

Rab kept his voice uncharacteristically low and told Murray, 'I'm glad you dropped by.' The phrase sounded stilted and old-fashioned, as if he'd accepted an invitation to afternoon tea. 'I felt that I might owe you an apology, for coming on too strong when I saw you last.'

Ray Costello folded his long body back on the bench beside Phylida, who shifted a little to make room for him.

'Are you turning exclusive, Robert?'

Rab grinned back.

'I think that the boy here may be in search of some advice that only I can give. Advice of a romantic nature.'

Phylida snorted. Costello ignored her. He nodded sagely. 'The Romantics should be a young man's province, Rab. You and I are too old to understand the bravado of it. We don't have the energy any more, we're spent forces.'

Phylida muttered something, but Ray talked on. 'Take the funeral of Shelley, a complete palaver and yet at the same time one of the most beautiful moments in the history of English literature. The beach, the sunset, the burning pyre, the crumbling skull of the poet cradled in the hands of his friend.' His eyes took on that sad, dreamy look reserved for spaniels and old men on their third drink. 'When I die I request that you burn me on the beach at Ayr.'

Phylida snorted. 'And will your wife send letters begging for the return of your desiccated heart?'

'Christ, she ripped that from my chest long ago.'

The couple embarked on well-practised bickering and Lyle Joff stepped outside to use his mobile.

Rab leaned towards Murray. 'They've performed that routine more often than Flanders and Swan.' His face set into a stern inquisitiveness, eyebrows raised almost to the ridges of his brow. It was just acting. The look he gave nervous students to encourage them to speak up in tutorials. 'Still, it gives me the perfect opportunity to apologise. Just because I'm not getting any doesn't give me a right to become one of the moral majority. Shake?'

He held out his hand.

Murray had let slip about Rachel a month into the affair. The two men had eaten dinner with a visiting speaker, then gone for a drink on their own to discuss the lecture free of its author. Maybe it was the combination of wine and beer or maybe it was the rose-tinted evening. Maybe he was boasting or maybe just for that instant Murray had thought his friend might be able to help. Whatever it was, as they'd left the pub, skirting the exiled smokers loitering on the pavement outside and stepping into the gloaming of a pink sunset, Murray had found himself saying, 'I'm having a bit of a thing with Rachel Houghton.'

Purvis had been more forthright than a casual listener might expect a professor of Romantic poetry to be.

'She's a ballbreaker. I wouldn't touch her with a bargepole.'

Murray had glanced at his friend's tubby abdomen and tied to imagine Rachel propositioning Rab as she had him, shutting the door of his office on sports afternoon Wednesday, pushing the essays he'd been trawling through to one side, sitting on the edge of his desk, so close he'd wondered, then guiding his hand under her sweater so that the quality of his wonder had shifted and magnified.

'It wasn't a bargepole that I was thinking of.'

'Any kind of pole. Leave well alone, if you know what's good for you.'

'What if it's my one last chance of true love?'

'Then run for the hills. Rachel Houghton isn't looking for love, Murray. She's happy with Fergus. She just likes spicing things up by screwing around.'

'And what's wrong with that?'

'Nothing, if shagging your head of department's wife doesn't bother you.'

'Why should it?'

'Would you like me to give you a list?'

'Not really.'

But his friend had gone on to recite a long, frequently crude, but eminently sensible catalogue of reasons why Murray Watson should steer clear of Rachel Houghton. It hadn't made one iota of difference. The affair remained acknowledged but unmentioned again, until now.

Murray took Rab's proffered hand and shook it.

'She just dumped me.'

'Ah.' Rab sucked another inch off his pint. 'In that case I take back my apology. You're better off out of it. You know what the department's like. A busy little hive with bees swarming all over each other and Fergus at the centre, gobbling up the golden globules of honey we lay at his feet.'

'Pollen.'

'What?'

'Pollen – the bees bring the queen pollen and she makes it into honey.'

'Pollen, honey, it's all the same.' Rab abandoned the analogy. 'The place is a poisonous rumour mill. Look,' his voice took on the fatherly tone that indicated advice was about to be proffered, 'I know it's not easy working where we do.

It's like being a diabetic in a candy shop, all those delectable sweet things passing through your hands every day and you not even allowed the tiniest little lick.' He laughed. 'That was slightly filthier than I intended.'

'It's okay, I get your drift.'

'You don't have to tell me how frustrating it can be. When I started it was different, but ...' Rab drifted off for a moment to the happy land where lecturers and students were still compatible. 'But times change.' He sighed, staring into the middle distance. 'I was having a nice drink until you came in looking like Banquo's ghost and reminded me how everything has gone to shit. You had a good time and now it's over. Just thank whatever ancient gods it is you worship that you didn't get caught.'

'We did. Someone saw us.'

'Ah,' Rab sighed. 'I suppose that would put a different complexion on things.' He took another sip of his pint. 'Come on, then. Don't leave me in suspense. Who?'

'I don't know. Someone. A porter maybe. I had my back to them.'

'Spare me the gory details.' Rab grunted. 'I hope to god it wasn't a porter. They'll tell the cleaners, who'll let slip to the women in the canteen, and once it gets to them you're lost. Might as well take out a full page ad in the *Glasgow Herald*, except there'd be no need; they'd already have saved you the fee.' He shook his head. 'If you don't know who it was, you can't be sure there's a problem.'

'They didn't see us standing too close in the coffee lounge or exchanging notes in the quads. They saw me rogering her on the desk of my office.'

'Rogering?'

'Making "the beast with two backs", "putting the horns on old Fergus", or whatever you Romantics call it.'

'Shagging.'

'What do you think I should do?'

'What can you do?' Rab patted his arm. 'Get a round in.'

Fowlers had quenched thirsts for at least a hundred years. Its high ceiling was iced with intricate cornicing, its windows frosted with etchings advertising whiskies and beers, which let light filter into the bar, but allowed priests, poets, skivers, fathers-on-an-errand, or men seeing-about-dogs, recalcitrant students and lovers budgeting towards leaving their spouses, privacy from passers-by. Mrs Noon kept things tight and it was rare to wait too long to be served or to see a fight that got beyond the third punch. Fowlers should have been a nice place for a drink, but it was a dump, a prime contender for a brewery-theme-pub revamp. There were no ashtrays on the table, but the ceiling retained its nicotine hue and the smell of unwashed old men, stale beer and the cheap bleach used to sluice down the toilets was no longer masked by cigarette smoke. The barstools, which harboured men who remembered the city when it was all soot and horseshit, were as scuffed and unsteady on their pins as their occupants. The patterned orange and blue carpet, once loud enough to drown out the Saturday-night crowd, had sunk to sludge. Murray tipped back his fifth pint of the evening and decided that this was where he belonged.

Phylida and Ray had left an hour or so ago, taking their quarrel to one of the West End restaurants where they were known and dreaded. Phylida had had trouble getting her arm into the sleeve of her jacket and Murray had helped her, guiding her hand into the armhole while Ray strode to the door with the single-minded purpose of the practised inebriate.

'You're a lovely man, Murray. Take my advice.' She gathered her bags of shopping; ingredients for another Friday-night dinner she was destined not to cook. 'Never get involved with someone who isn't available.'

'What made you say that, Phylida?'

'I don't know.' She gave a silly grin. 'I have been drinking, you know.'

Now there were three of them left. Lyle Joff, quieter after his phone call, Rab and Murray. They were still at the corner table, but in the hours they had sat there the pub had transformed from a peaceful place where men could swap confidences into a red-faced rammy. The bar was three deep, the staff quick-pouring wine and pressing more glasses to optics than they had earlier in the evening, but it was still pints that ruled; a shining spectrum of gold, yellows, browns and liquorice black. Not that anyone stopped to admire their drink. There was no holding it in the air, marvelling at the head on it, watching the sweat dribble down the glass before lifting it to your lips and taking a long swallow, your pronounced, but not disgusting, just perfectly manly, Adam's apple bobbing pleasingly up and down. People were knocking them back faster than it was possible to serve and from time to time a barmaid would squeeze into the throng and return with a tall pile of tumblers, as if gathering ammunition for a siege.

Two thoughts were pinballing around Murray's brain. The first was his need for another drink, the magic one that would make everything click into place. The second was that he'd drunk too much and should get home before he shipwrecked himself.

Maybe it was the bell that made him think of shipwrecks. It was loud and clanging and spoke to him of treacherous rocks and shattered hulks. What was it like to drown?

'Pushing the boat out tonight?'

That's what they were doing, setting out into perilous waters, and none of them in possession of their sea legs.

Murray raised his head. Mrs Noon was holding a tin tray loaded with empty tumblers, their rims edged with tides of dead froth. He wasn't sure he'd ever seen the woman out from behind the bar before.

'I didn't know you had legs, Mrs Noon.' He grinned. 'I thought you were a mermaid. Great singers, mermaids. They lure poor sailors to their deaths, just for the fun of it. Beautiful creatures, beautiful and cruel.'

'You wouldn't want to hear me sing.' The manageress placed his half-full glass in amongst the empties on her tray. 'That really would be a cruelty.' She watched Rab neck the dregs of his pint, then took his glass from him. 'Time to head home, gentlemen.'

She was right. They should have left hours ago. Now here he was, drunk and sober at the same time. Each half of him disgusted at the other.

Someone had propped the doors open. The crowd was thinning, people sinking the last of their drinks, reaching for their jackets, all the heat and chatter drifting out into the night. He stretched an arm towards his beer, but Mrs Noon sailed the tray up and away, beyond his reach.

'What happened to drinking-up time?'

It came out too loud, an aggressive beggar's bleat. He caught the barman throwing Mrs Noon a look and the woman's answering shake of the head.

'You heard the bell – that's drinking-up time over. Do you want to get me into trouble?'

He was a lecturer in English literature at a distinguished and ancient university. He straightened himself in his chair and summoned forth the spirit of Oscar Wilde.

'Don't you think you may be a little old for me to get you into trouble, Mrs Noon?'

'No need for that now.' Rab was pulling on his jacket. 'You'll have to excuse my colleague. He is the recipient of bad news.'

Murray lumbered to his feet. The battle was lost, there was no more drink to be had, no possibility of reaching the required state here. The landlady disregarded Rab's apologies and turned her practised smile on Murray: ice and glass. She'd once told him she had a daughter at the Uni.

'I was just thinking the same thing of the pair of you. You're both a little old to be getting into trouble.'

Outside, black cabs and private hires edged along the road accompanied by the bass beat and infra-bright lights of sober boys in zooped-up cars. It was another kind of rush hour, Friday-night chucking-out time, louder, younger and messier than the into-work-and-home-again crowds. Here came the smashed windows, spilled noodles, lost shoes and sicked-up drinks, the pigeon breakfasts and trailing bloodstains.

Two teenage girls perched on the windowsill of the late-night Spar passing a bottle between them while a yard away their friend snogged a youth in a tracksuit, their joined mouths sealed vacuum tight. The boy's hand slid up the girl's crop top. One of the drinkers tipped back a swig from the bottle, arching her body theatrically, her short skirt riding up her thighs. For an instant she looked like an advert for the elixir of youth. Then she lost her balance and bumped against her companion. Both girls giggled and the one who had nearly fallen shouted, 'Fucking jump him if you're gonnae, or we'll miss the bus.'

The boy broke the clinch, grinning at his audience, then pulled the girl back to him, whispering something that made her laugh, then push herself free, staggering slightly on her high heels as she tottered towards her friends.

'Virgin,' the teenagers taunted, passing her the bottle.

Lyle Joff gave them a stern look. 'I should bloody hope so.' The girls sniggered, nudging each other and Lyle took refuge in his kebab. He didn't speak again until they had passed the group.

'If I caught Sarah or Emma behaving like that, I'd lock them up until they were thirty. Fuck it, thirty-five. I'd lock them up till they were thirty-five and even then I'd still want some guarantees.'

Murray looked back at the girls. They were at the bus stop now. One of them – he wasn't sure if it was the one who'd been doing the kissing – pushed the boy. The youth stepped into a half-trot, shouting something. The girls roared back, united now as they rushed at him, their high heels clattering against the pavement, laughing, full of victory as the boy ran off down the street.

Murray joined in the laughter. Some people just had more of a talent for life.

'*Brief Encounter*.'

'It's not funny, Murray. Boys like that, they take advantage of young girls.'

Rab asked, 'What age are Sarah or Emma now? Five and seven? You don't need to worry about that for a few years.'

'Three and six. Remind me to look up good convent schools in the Yellow Pages in the morning. Here, hold this a minute.'

Lyle thrust his half-eaten kebab into Murray's hand and nipped up a lane. Murray lifted the swaddled meat and salad to his mouth, crunching into vinegar, spices and heat. When had he last eaten? There had been a packet of crisps in the pub, but before that? Some sauce escaped the wrap and ran down his chin.

'Hey.' Lyle emerged from the alleyway. 'I said hold it, not eat it.'

'Sorry.' Murray wiped his face. He took a second bite, then handed it back. 'I don't know how you can stomach that stuff.'

Lyle tore at the kebab with his teeth, then held it in front of them, like a prime specimen in a lecture. 'Repast of kings and sultans – you've got all your main food groups in this. Your protein ...' – he selected a slither of grey meat and held it up for inspection before dropping it into his mouth – '... your veggies, your carbohydrate, and a tincture of roughage.' Lyle fed the end of the kebab into his mouth and started picking at the shreds of salad and onion left in the paper. 'I used to live on these before Marcella got her claws into me.'

His expression looked like it might crumple and he shoved the kebab into his mouth again, as if seeking solace.

They were passing the queue for The Viper Club now. Murray recognised a girl from his third-year tutorial group. She'd caught her long, straight hair back in an Alice band. Her dress was short, her white boots high. She made him think of the test-card girl, all grown up and gone kinky.

'Hello, Dr Watson.'

He nodded, trying not to stagger. Ah, what the fuck? He was allowed a private life wasn't he?

Rab echoed his thoughts. 'Sometimes you need to cut loose, connect with the elemental, remind yourself of the beauty of your own existence.'

Lyle scrunched the kebab's wrapping into a ball and tossed it into a bin already brimming with rubbish. 'For tomorrow we may die.' The paper trembled on the peak of the pile, then tumbled to the ground.

Rab bent over, picked up the wrapping and stuffed it carefully back into the bin. A look of satisfaction at a job well done settled on his face.

'Right, what den of iniquity are we headed to next?'

Murray surveyed the Viper's queue, catching sight of another familiar face. He grinned.

'What about here? Forget lining up with the plebs, Robbie old boy. I happen to have a connection.'

'I'm sorry, Dr Watson, but you wouldn't thank me tomorrow if I let you in tonight.' It was the third time she'd said no.

'C'mon, Murray. You heard the lassie. She's only doing her job.' Lyle stepped away from the door of the club and began walking towards the corner where Rab was already impatiently looking for an empty cab, but Murray stood his ground.

'I think I'm old enough to decide that for myself.'

The bouncer shuffled her feet against the pavement. Someone had made the shape of a heart on the concrete out of squashed-up dods of chewing gum. Students, he supposed, or maybe it was an art project. He was finding it increasingly difficult to distinguish contemporary art from a stupid waste of time.

The girl gave him a conciliatory smile.

'Come back tomorrow and I'll wheech you to the top of the queue, five-star treatment, but there's no way I can let you in tonight.'

Lyle had drifted back. 'C'mon. We'll away and find a pool hall.'

Murray ignored him. He'd taught her when? Three years ago? More, maybe. Ciara … Karen … Kirsty. She'd been a good student, conscientious, a feel for the subject. She could have gone on, done a postgrad perhaps.

'We're just looking for a last drink.'

'Not tonight. I'm sorry.'

The anger was like a physical thing. So hot in his chest he felt he could cough it up, like a giant greb.

A fucking drink. Was that too much to ask? Just a fucking pint of pishy lager.

It wasn't her fault. He shook his head, forcing a grin, and saw her relief. He wasn't going to make a fuss.

'C'mon, Murray.' Lyle's voice was insistent; he hadn't cottoned on yet that it was okay, all danger passed.

'Aye, aye. Let's go.'

'Dr Watson?' The bouncer's smile was kinder than the

pub landlady's, but it was undercut with the same disappointment. 'You should away home to bed now.'

He grinned. 'Not much point in that.'

A taxi stopped, depositing a shiny young couple onto the street. Murray gave a shout to Rab, then put his hand on Lyle's shoulder and steered him towards it. Kirsty smiled at the driver, reassuring him that appearances lied and the three men would be no bother.

Murray turned halfway in and almost lost his balance. 'For tomorrow we may die.'

The girl leaned into the cab. 'True enough, but do me a favour and make sure it's not tonight.'

She slammed the door, then ran back to her post. Murray saw her watching them as they sailed on into the night.

The thin man with the long hair and the bandana wanted a pound before he would let them in. Rab dropped three coins into the old ice-cream tub that acted as a till and they went up the stairs and into the electric brightness of the pool hall.

'I should head back.' It had been Lyle Joff's mantra since he'd phoned his wife two hours ago, but he joined the queue for the bar with the others and accepted his pint. 'Just the one, thanks. I'll need to be thinking about getting home.'

The room was busy with the quiet clack of billiard balls and the low murmur of conversation. They were in the first wave of pub exiles, and serious pool players still out-numbered those for whom the hall was just another stop on the night's drunken highway. It was about a year since Murray had been here, a night on the town with his brother Jack, but it was as if he'd just stepped out to take a piss. There were the same faces, the same closed looks and poker expressions. The same mix of scruff and cowboy-cool, the lavvy-brush beards, arse-hugging jeans, Cuban heels and tight-fitting waistcoats. Fuck, you'd have to be hard to wear that gear in Glasgow.

Rab lowered himself behind a free table. 'Welcome to Indian country. What time does this place stay open till?'

'Three.'

Rab's sigh was contented, nothing to worry about for two hours.

Joff stared silently at his pint as if it might hold the possi-bility of enlightenment. Slowly his head sunk onto his chest and his eyes closed.

A woman bent across the baize, lining up her options. Murray found himself following the seams of her jeans, up the inside of her raised thigh to the point where they met in a cross. He looked away. Would the tyranny of sex never stop?

He nodded towards Lyle. 'Is he all right?'

The woman telescoped her wooden cue back towards their table and Rab shifted his drink beyond its reach.

'He's fine. He'll wake up in a moment.' Rab indicated a trio of women sitting near the back of the room. 'Why don't you go over there and ask one of them if she wants a drink?'

Two of the trio could have been sisters, or maybe it was just that their style was the same. Strappy tops and short feathery hair whose copper highlights glinted under the bright lights. The third was draped in something baggy that was probably intended to camouflage her bulk, but made her body into a formless mass, a mountain on which her small head rested. They were grown-up versions of the girls he'd gone to school with. They'd never have looked at him then, but now?

It was stupid. He didn't fancy any of them; besides he wasn't up to the aggressive dance of tease and semi-insults that constituted a chat-up.

'They've got drinks.'

'Well, get up, pretend you're going to the Gents and offer them another one en route.'

'Is that how James Bond does it? Hello, ladies, I was just on my way for a pish and wondered if I could bring you anything back? Ever wondered why it's going to say "confirmed bachelor" on your obituary?'

'It must be better than mooning over Ms Houghton.'

Lyle Joff awakened slowly like an ugly toy twitching into life in a deserted nursery. The flesh beneath his eyes twitched and then the eyes themselves opened. He blinked and turned his fuzzy gaze on Murray.

'Rachel Houghton.' He smiled dreamily. 'Good arse. Good everything else, too.'

'Lyle.' Rab's voice was warning. 'We're talking about a colleague.'

Lyle's brief sleep seemed to have refreshed him. He wiped away the glue of saliva that had formed at the corners of his mouth and took a sip of his pint. 'Listen to Professor PC.'

Rab said, 'Shut up, Lyle. You're drunk.'

A couple of the pool players looked over. Murray raised his beer to his lips. It tasted of nothing.

'We're all drunk. Say what you were going to say, Lyle.'

'Lyle, I'm warning you.'

Rab's tone was low and commanding, but Lyle was too far gone to notice. He patted Rab's shoulder.

'Murray's one of us, the three mouseketeers.' He giggled. 'It's top secret. Rab said Fergus would have his balls strung up and made into an executive toy for his desk if he found out.'

'The three musketeers, great swordsmen.' Murray turned to Rab. 'What's the big secret?'

'Nothing. Lyle's just being provocative, aren't you, Lyle?'

'Not as provocative as Rachel.' Lyle put an arm around Rab. 'I wouldn't have thought you had it in you.'

Rab lifted the arm from his shoulder. His eyes met Murray's and all of the ruined adventure was in them. There was no need to ask what had happened, but Murray said, 'Tell me.'

Lyle looked from one to the other, wary as a barroom dog whose master is on his fourth drink.

Rab sighed wearily. 'What's the point? She's a free spirit, Murray. A generous woman.'

'I want to know.'

A little beer had slopped onto the table. Rab dipped his finger in it and drew a damp circle on the Formica. He looked his age.

'A one-off mercy fuck – that's all there is to it.'

'When?'

'The end of last term. You remember all that hoo-ha about my introduction to the new Scottish poetry anthology?'

Murray did. Rab had been forthright in his assessment that Scotland was entering a golden wave of poetry by throwing off the class-consciousness, self-obsession and non-poetic subject matter of a previous generation. The new wave had leapt to the defence of their predecessors while baulking at Rab's description of them as non-political. The elder statesmen had been vitriolic in their condemnation of academics in general and Rab in particular. It must have been a week when war and disaster had slipped from the news, because the row had hit the broadsheets. Rab had been almost universally derided by academics and pundits north of the border and a source of amusement to those south of it.

'It all blew up in my face a bit. Some people thrive on controversy – Fergus, for example – but I don't. It got me down. Rachel dropped into my office one afternoon to commiserate and we went for a few drinks, quite a few drinks. Then when the pub closed I remembered that there was another bottle at my place. There's always another bottle at my place.' He gave a sad smile. 'I didn't expect her to come, and then when she did I didn't expect anything more than a drink. I was going to tell you.' He laughed almost shyly. 'But a gentleman doesn't talk about these things.'

'You bloody talked about it to Lyle.'

'Oh come on, Murray. I'm an overweight fifty-year-old poetry lecturer and Rachel's a thirty-five-year-old dolly bird. I had to tell someone. Anyway, I'd been drinking.'

'You've generally been drinking.'

'That's a prime example of why I didn't tell you. You can be such a fucking puritan. I thought you wouldn't approve.' He gave a low laugh. 'And then you told me that you and she … well I was jealous, I admit, but not jealous enough to throw it back in your face.' Rab raised his pint to his lips and then wiped his mouth on the back of his hand. His tone slipped from apologetic to defensive. 'I don't see what you're getting so hot under the collar for, anyway. She's another man's wife. She doesn't belong to you, me or anyone else in the department she might have fucked, except maybe Fergus, and if so I'd say he's doing a very poor job of holding on to his property.'

It was the female player's turn again. Rab moved his drink as she pulled the cue back, then fired a red ball across the baize. Murray watched it sail into the depths of a corner pocket, sure as death.

He imagined taking the pool cue from her hand and smashing it into Rab Purvis's beer-shined face. Teeth first, then nose. He'd leave the eyes alone. He'd always been squeamish about that kind of thing.

Lyle said, 'Are you okay, Murray?'

He didn't answer, just got to his feet and left before any more damage could be done.

He had been walking for a long time. Once a police car slowed and took a look at him, he ignored them and they drove on past, but their interest seemed to be the signal for his feet to start a winding route home. He was in the confluence of wide, lonely streets that made up Park Circus now. Sometime after parlour maids and footmen decided they'd rather risk their health in munitions factories or the battlefield, the smart residences had been converted into hotels and offices. Now they'd been deserted for city centre lets and were slowly being reclaimed by speculative builders. Murray wandered past the weathered 'To Let' signs, not registering the sycamore shoots sprouting from neglected guttering, the broken railings and chipped steps that might tumble the unsuspecting into the dank courtyards of window-barred basements. But the plague town atmosphere of the shuttered houses and empty streets suited his mood.

He took his mobile from his pocket and accessed the number he had taken from a list in the front office and stupidly promised himself he'd never use. The night was starting to turn. He'd reached the edge of Kelvingrove Park and birds were beginning to sing to each other. Murray pressed 'Call' and waited while his signal bounced around satellites stationed in the firmament above, or whatever it did in that pause before the connection was made. He let it ring until an automated voice told him the person he was looking for was unavailable, then hung up and pressed 'Redial'. This time the other end picked up and Professor Fergus Baine's voice demanded, 'Do you know what time it is?'

Murray cut the call. He sat on a wall and listened to the birds celebrating the return of the sun, then after a minute or two his phone vibrated into the stupid jingle he'd never bothered to change. He took it out, glanced at caller display and saw the unfamiliar number flashing on the screen.

'Hello?' His voice was slurred.

'Is that you, Murray?' Fergus sounded wide awake. Did he never sleep? 'What do you want? Something urgent, I imagine?'

'I wanted to speak to Rachel.'

It was ridiculous, all of it; stupid.

'Rachel is asleep. Perhaps you can call back in the morning?' The professor's politeness was damning.

Somewhere in the recesses of Murray's brain was the knowledge that now was the time to quit, while he still had the slim chance of writing the call off as a drunken indiscretion. But in the morning he would have lost his courage.

'I need to talk to her now.'

'Well, you can't. Call back at a decent hour.'

The line went dead.

Murray stood and soberly surveyed the sunrise. A door in the empty street opened and some partygoers reeled out, their voices high and excited. A young girl drifted over and put an arm around his shoulder.

'Look, Dr Watson.' She pointed unsteadily across the parkland. 'Isn't it beautiful?'

The sun was fully up now and only a few streaks of pink remained smeared against the blue. The light caught against the trees, shifting their leaves all the greens and yellows in the spectrum. The birds had ceased their revels and calm had settled. Even the concrete hulk of hospital buildings in the distance seemed at one with the day. Murray looked at the new-minted morning and agreed that, yes, it really was beautiful.

Calculus

DIRAN ADEBAYO is a London-born novelist, cultural critic and broad-caster. His debut novel, *Some Kind of Black*, won him numerous awards, and was longlisted for the Booker Prize. Its follow-up, *My Once Upon a Time*, which he describes as a 'latter day Pilgrim's Progress', fused film noir and fairytale with Yoruba myth. 'Calculus' is a work-in-progress from his third novel, *The Ballad of Dizzy and Miss P* – 'a tale of race, sex, science and New Britain' scheduled for publication in 2010.

AT MY DOOR, SOMETHING CHANGED, maybe before. I'm fiddling for my key when he leans forward and cheek-kisses me lightly. 'Alright. I'm gone,' he said. 'You're okay from here, yeah?' It sounds fine saying it, even then he sounded pleasant enough, but there was an opaqueness, a slight hardness in his eyes that had always shone warm and clear with me. He made a 'phone' gesture with his hand to his ear before disappearing down the stairs.

It felt abrupt, this leaving. He muttered something about some work he had to do, which seemed unlikely. I had the distinct impression he was irked with me and I couldn't imagine why, or when. That, and the walk back, sobered me up, so though I put a bucket by my bed, just in case, I doubted I would need it.

I thought on it more the next day, the end. I could recall us passing a couple of acquaintances as we entered the hall – this girl I knew to talk to. I didn't even think I'd said

159

anything. Maybe the merest thing and we'd walked on. It occurred to me, too, that he still hadn't properly touched me. He could have tried to put his arm around me on the walk back, say. I was pretty sure he hadn't.

I don't know, I felt … not quite let down by him, but whatever's less. I was terse when he called.

'How you feeling?' he asked. Fine, I replied. 'You had some Coke? It's good for a hangover.' I said, no, I hadn't.

'You still up for Outcaste Tuesday?'

'What?'

'You know. My friend's club. We talked about it.'

I didn't remember, and I wasn't mad about clubs. He said this one was different, trust him. I ummed and could definitely hear agitation in his voice. I said I was real busy for the Wednesday. That I had work, like he'd said he had.

I did go. Didn't wear anything especial, though, just jeans, and didn't cut my hair either, kept the cap on. Fitted in fine, as it turned out – most were pretty dressed down in there, trainers, and tops tied round their backs and whatever, plus the place itself was quite rough-and-ready – this disused basement feel. Dark and bare stone walls and different rooms.

I liked how walking through felt like wandering through caves, and this music, Indian meets drum'n'bassy, new and interesting to me, then being ushered into this further, chill-out space, for his friend Salim's tightest, and tequila tumblers, him going, 'This is my friend Colette,' then glancing me these certain looks, like a query, and being chatted to by Salim's girlfriend Christy especially.

She was nice, no superiors, talked like we were gonna be mates, you know. Worked as a magician at kids' and office parties, which was a bit more down to earth, in a way, than I'd expected. I thought, they're not so beyond, his cool people. Very low-key with Salim, I noticed; you wouldn't have known they were together necessarily, and that made me feel a bit better about before, just seeing how understated was in his circle. And when she assumed about us, raising her eyes at me when we spotted the two of them doing shady in a corner, like 'Our Boys!', I swelled inside, and realised I'd all but forgotten about reducing him in my mind.

I couldn't work out what she was. She looked Asian mixed African. There were all these different Asians about: his what he'd call 'boho' types and then the black-strutting SOAS variety. At one point these two I recognised from the poolside posse hovered by the curtain to our bit, desperate for an entrée, and it did tickle me, this new position. How I'd vaulted past. Just maybe.

And then Björk sauntered through! This slip of a thing in a white smock, with this big DJ I hadn't heard of. This was where she came for ideas, apparently. I was a bit 'Wow!'

I must admit. I was really quite into her, you know, at the time.

A bunch of us headed back to the dancefloors, after her. Didn't see her dance, but got bopping a bit with Christy to this tune I'd been hearing in the halls, tabla'd up. Surprised myself – I did like dancing when I did it, just didn't do it much, and less since I'd been up here. I like it when it's – not when it's posey but it's just dealing with energy, and this felt good, with this pent-up-ness inside, and Christy, people, just dancing different ways. There didn't seem any official moves yet.

He finished with his buttonhole, and took up beside me, tumbler in hand, rocking a bit.

'How's my friend Colette?' he asked. 'Still mad at me? Cos you've been a little bit. No? Can't think why!'

An innocent's wonder on his face. A teasey fringe, though, like he suspected the subject area really.

I couldn't hold his gaze. Not whilst he knew and I didn't. Just wanting to know: for myself, of course, to confirm these new funs true, but as well just to beat the tease. Reduce his advantage, make us evens again.

'No?'

I punched at his midriff. Quite hard, actually.

'You dance like you walk. Quick,' he grinned.

I punched at him again, and he caught my hand with his free one. Held it and was looking at me searchingly, like trying to guess me. I swelled and my breath came out in a hiccupy gasp, how it can sometimes. I could see him inching and I closed my eyes, and felt it. Smelt his face by my neck and felt it again. He dropped my arm down, slipped his other around, restarted us slowly, and all last battlings were going.

We had a proper snog back at mine. It was really nice and everything, getting a proper feel of him, but I wasn't about to do what comes next, just like that, and he was getting a touch forward in my belt area. I don't know if he saw it in my eyes, but he tailed off and I went to the bathroom. And when I came back it was different: the stereo was playing and his eyes were shining.

'You got this! Fuck, man – you got this!'

He had a CD case in one hand and both arms were up, to the music. It was this Saint-Saëns symphony, No. 3, that I'd been playing earlier, that I'd left in the machine.

'This bit. They used this for a pop song in the seventies. My folks used to have it. I can't believe you've got this.'

It'd been one of, like, three pop songs his parents had had when he was a kid. Three little 45s tucked away in this big seventies radiogram. He hadn't heard it for ever.

I sat on the bed and listened properly. It was the choral variation on the main melody, stately organ, trumpets and strings scaling to this grand crescendo. Quite famous – probably the most famous bit.

'Wasn't this a hymn?' I said.

'I don't think so.' He wouldn't be denied. 'This is the only other time I've heard it.'

He was beaming at me his biggest, strangest yet. Reverently, like I was ... I don't know, like 'Eureka'.

I snort-laughed it away, then proper giggled when he began singing the tune, his version. He was right – what he'd said before: his voice was shocking. Creaky and way flat. But he looked so sincere, sort-of-committed, doing it – it was sweet!

He plopped down beside me, abashed, started scrutinising the liner notes, so I started humming it. I hadn't meant to stop him. He was nodding, head down, then considered me, and it was 'Eureka' time again, mild version. We met in between and it was just this great kiss. A thank you kiss, it felt like, with knobs on. Kinda chaste. Not hot and hungry, like before, but eaten already; soft and savouring and certain. An old kiss.

He let go of my hand, looked sad all of a sudden.

'No, it just makes me funny to hear this,' he said. 'Some stuff just makes you want to bawl your eyes out and you don't know why. Sometimes, you know, memories and what-not, but sometimes it's just, ah, you see what you lack,

I think. You wish your life could be like that. Whether it's good or sad.'

'Music, man!' He got up, sighing, shaking his head. 'It's top dog. You can direct people, make everybody get your thing, but still leave space for heads. Drawing, writing, it's hard to bring your full thing.'

'But that's your job, isn't it? Making people see your "things". I mean,' I felt quite tired for this, 'isn't it?'

'Indeed.' He laughed. 'Tough girl!'

He wanted to know how to program the machine so it would repeat the section. I hadn't really used those buttons and I stretched out whilst he went away to fiddle, thinking he'd settle back for seconds of the last one. But he'd just come to share something excited, then disappear to scan for more good bits, and back then forth, before questions about orchestras, and something over his shoulder, in his quantum dimension, all fleshly energies transferred. Funny boy, I thought, again, how you switch.

I didn't mind, though. Still quite cosy: him showing his signs of relaxed, all a-fizz to this stuff I'd imagined counting against me. Just how he was, I think, this feeling he gave that you were seeing the real somebody, made me believe the best bits, the kiss and the look before, that bit more.

I dozed off – he must have disappeared some time – and when I awoke day was breaking. He'd draped a blanket over me and was sketching something, still on that movement.

He called the next day to say, guess what, his flatmate was gonna be away that weekend, and did I want to come down for food and 'general chill'. I said that sounds nice.

I went to the salon and Sandra did have various thoughts but in the end I settled on a trim. I wore my navy blue blouse and this long silk skirt, split at the calf so a hint of leg, that my mum got me from the store where she works. Just to stress, I guess, adult material: that I could do lady, too.

I had to practise walking around in it 'cos it cramped my step a bit. (Mum would have been happy!) Then packed my little face kit, and a bottle of wine, and my toothbrush, finally.

I hadn't decided exactly. I just thought, we'll see.

We played chess perched in the kitchen whilst he cooked. Our first game! It was funny – both of us a bit trying to outdo each other with how long it'd been since we'd last played. Still, it wasn't a bad one, standard-wise, till he made a careless move in mid-game, putting his queen in a pinnable position and, shortly after, he flicked his king over. I did offer to let him take the queen move back, which I wouldn't obviously normally, and we could restart from there, but he said, 'Course not. You won fair and square. One–nil.'

Food was delish. Rice, chicken and okra in this thick spicy soup plus these yummy 'do-do' slices – fried plantain, another first – and then after we settled in his room on the rugs on his bed on the floor. Zillions of books and videos and records and comics – and he showed me this series from his portfolio, these sort of comic-style recreations of historical situations. So much to know, it hit home, does he really not mind?

Mainly we reminisced on the first times. I told him how I'd had headphones on at the SOAS bar as people-deterrent, and he admitted he had been a bit pissed with me that first date, at the end. 'You're a sharp one,' he said; he didn't think he'd shown it. Not pissed off exactly, just, well, you see he'd had a really good feeling about me already, and mmm, he'd been minded to express that some way – Wanted to, and you didn't, I cut him. That's games. You said you don't play games. He didn't, he replied, he'd said I don't play games. But it wasn't a game. Come on, I was drunk, badder than he'd realised, and say we had kissed he wouldn't have felt good 'cos there wouldn't have been proper consent, my side. And when you have that feeling especially, it had to start right. Say we get married and Man's asking him 'How did you start?' and he says 'Well, she was drunk and I took advantage.' What kind of a low-class story would that be?

Tell me about the feeling, I stroked him. Oh, it had to be a strong one. You think I'd approach just any yout? Watch it, I poked him. It was a proper feeling, a tad dented as you seesawed up your stairs. But then we hit Salim's thing, and you were settling down with his girl and generally acquitting yourself robustly. If I was off somewhere you were cool. Then going back to yours and you had my song! And it was symphony number three – three's one of my lucky numbers, plus then your name, Colette, seven letters – seven's my other lucky one. And that was it! A done deal, in my head.

Seven's a silly reason, I said. I'm adopted. It's not my ... real name. Adopted is seven too, he came back. Seven's a silly reason. No, no, you check it out. Seven's very big in the world. All the religions have something about seven. The Bible – seven sacraments, seven years of famine, then seven years of fat. Isn't it the number of completion or something? And, to be fair, it was true that some numbers are sort of bigger than others, like pi, and 1.618, etc., you know that proportion by which each bone in human fingers is bigger than the one before, and other ratios that keep cropping up in nature. And seven was a little special, in that respect. It's a prime, and I remembered something this teacher said about tides – about how the real, proper waves come in primes, the first one then the third, etc., and that the biggest one was always the seventh. Plus a lot of allergies, like asthma, go after seven years. We speculated that seven might be the rhythm of life, and he leant over to play this really pretty soul tune of that name. I hadn't much liked soul before.

Twenty-six, I piped up, twenty-six is important too. That's the number, the atomic number for iron, which is the most stable element, the most common thing out there. It's perfectly balanced between all the different forces. In nature, everything aspires to the stability of iron.

He frowned a bit at this. Couldn't see how it fitted; how you could make a three or a seven from it. Ah leave it, he gave up – who wants to be common anyway?

'... It feels a bit ... I don't know. All these tests!'

'Flying colours!' He kissed me with a plop. 'The rhythms of life, your tapeless walkman. Move – I'm learning already! That's why we do it, no? Relationships. New information.'

It felt like we'd eaten already again. Having the afters, the talking afters, before the main course. Just lying and leafing, and touching and exploring, and challenging and tickling and irritating; talking when we wanted, and messing when we didn't. And more secure, and more and more hot, and more bits off ... till you know what!

Everything smooth till he was actually inside. I'd let him in naked 'cos he said he wouldn't get hard otherwise, and you don't need much persuading at that stage. So we're rocking away, and it's a bit big, but okay, and he goes, 'Mm!

You know that pain I had. I'm not feeling it at all!' and, at the sudden remembrance, I closed up, shooting him out. He grunted and looked at me startled, then chuckled, then me too. Anyway, we wrapped him up – that was a song and dance. 'Are you sure you've done this before?' I asked him – and I escorted it back in, only he's really struggling now to stay strong like before. And whenever he's getting there, I push and expel him. I was pissing myself 'cos he'd be pumping, pumping, eyes closed, really trying, then glance at me suspiciously, his dick receding in anticipation.

He made me promise not to do it any more, but he was still struggling. Then he mutters, short, fast breaths, 'Say me your A Levels!' 'What?' 'A Levels, A Levels!' 'Double Maths, Physics, Biology.' 'Double! Shit! Oh shit, that's so hardcore! And again, baby.' 'Double Maths, Physics, Biology,' I laughed. 'No, no – seriously! ... Oh shit! Yup! That's great!'

Maybe it did do the trick, 'cos he got there this time, just in time. I was having trouble restraining myself. I left it seven seconds, then pushed as quick and as hard as I could. 'Oww!' he moaned, clenching it as he fell away. 'It's tender, man! Not funny.' But it was, all was. This is what sex should be like, I thought. I think I was a bit in love with him already.

Trouble in Paradise

AUTHOR'S NOTE
When *Bridget Jones's Diary* was published in the mid-1990s there was a fair amount of fuss about the fact that the whole thing seemed to be rather shallow and silly. Occasionally I felt moved to point out that my first novel, *Cause Celeb*, had been set in a refugee camp in the Sudan but nobody bought that one. Actually I never intended to write *Bridget Jones's Diary* at all. When it started as a column in the *Independent*, I was toiling on my second novel, *Trouble in Paradise* – a story set in a luxury resort on a banana-growing island. It was about the reasons people from the Western world go on these holidays: what they are escaping and what they are hoping to find; the lives of the people who work in the hotel; and how the two interact. This excerpt comes from near the beginning. I have left it in its early stage but it kind of fits with the idea of *Ox-Tales*.

HELEN FIELDING, born in Morley, West Yorkshire, is best known as the author of *Bridget Jones's Diary* (winner of the British Book of the Year Award, 1998) and its sequel *Bridget Jones: The Edge of Reason*. Her most recent book was a spy spoof, *Olivia Joules and the Overactive Imagination*.

1

SIMON PRENDEGAST SWAM AS FAR into the shallows as he could before he grounded his stomach on the sandy bottom, then stood up suddenly in water that only came halfway up his shins – a trick which had given him pleasure for three decades. He pulled in his stomach as he made his way up the beach to the hotel. He was tall, thin, sixty, crusted by the sun. The Spice Island was under-occupied at the moment, it being November, and only just out of the rains. He followed his usual route, across the lawn, past the sign saying 'Do not molest the plants' and around the lagoon pool, noting with pleasure that, though already 8.30am, only three or four of the sunloungers had towels on them. Down the beach, the Half Moon Bay had built a separate hotel for Germans, which amused Prendegast enormously.

Hyacinth approached, her magnificent bottom splendid in a straight petrol-blue skirt, with the Tradewinds regulation parrot-spattered shirt on top. She wore a gold badge bearing her name, so that, as Prendegast had pointed out when Tradewinds launched the badges at an 'employee event', the guests were better equipped to patronise and complain about the staff.

'Mr Prendegast,' said Hyacinth. 'Mr Kyam want speak with you.' Hyacinth, a handsome woman, could have been anything between forty and sixty.

'With little me? Oh, Hyacinth. My heart it soars like an eagle.'

She let out a deep laugh. 'Oh boy, Mr Prendegast. There going be trouble if he do continue in this manner.'

'Oh God. What is it now?'

'Oh boy,' said Hyacinth shaking her head. 'Oh boy.'

Prendegast made his way up to his cottage at the top of the hill, with its panoramic view of Grand Anse beach and the islands. He showered off quickly and dressed in pale blue slacks, a white shirt and a denim sailor's cap, then he made his way back down the steep coral path which wound its way through the greenery, giving glimpses of extraordinary shades of blue water. When he reached what used to be his office, he opened the door without knocking, to be greeted by a freezing blast from the air conditioning. Kyam was sitting at the desk, writing, and did not look up.

'Good God, Kyam, it's like an arsing deep freeze in here. What's the matter with you? I hope you're wearing a vest.'

Kyam continued to write, pettily. He had made it perfectly clear that he expected everyone, including Prendegast, to knock. A management whizz from Houston, he was a very clean twenty-eight-year-old of Chinese extraction. He was short, and tending to fat. Eventually he laid down his pen, and looked up. 'Thank you for making the time to see me, sir,' he said.

'Well, you know, it was tricky, but I managed to force you a window,' said Prendegast.

'We have a problem ... er, an opportunity, with the staff.'

'Really, Kyam? And what might that be?' said Prendegast. The financial collapse of his hotel, which had been a sort of barefoot rich man's hangout, was widely attributed to: a) his drinking, and b) his management style – described by Tradewinds as 'gone native'. At the takeover Prendegast had been appointed Executive Consultant – a title as lacking in meaning as it was remuneration. Tradewinds had supplied him with a procession of managers, whom Prendegast had systematically reduced to shadows of their former selves, culminating in the appointment, two months ago, of the automaton-like Kyam.

'It's the fish, sir. Fish.'

'What about the fish? You've had an opportunity with some fish?'

'The staff have been obtaining fish' – *abtynin furssh*, he pronounced it – 'from the ocean, sir.'

Prendegast hated the way Kyam called him 'sir'. He believed it to be the product of eight weeks' deliberation at a residential management course in Scottsdale, Arizona.

'They have been placing the fish in the freezer,' Kyam continued. 'For reasons of hygiene, I have deemed it necessary to prevent the employees from deploying the fish in the said' – *seyud* – 'manner. This has created an opportunity.'

'An arpordooonideee, Kyam? Or an apordunidooodeee?'

'I believe you heard what I said, sir.'

'You're talking about the staff fishing off the jetty in their breaks? To supplement your inadequate wages.'

'That ... that is correct. That is to say, the fishing is the matter in question.'

'You haven't stopped them fishing?'

'Not exactly, sir.'

'So what's the problem?'

'It's the placing of the fish in the refrigerator or freezer which is the difficulty.'

'What's wrong with that?'

'Hygiene, sir.'

'Well, can't they put the fish in polythene bags?'

'It's against regulations, sir. Only items ordered and cleared through the ordering system may be placed in the deep freeze.'

'They're catching the fish to take home and eat. They can't leave it lying in the sun to rot all day. Where else are they supposed to keep it?'

'There's another situation we need to discuss, sir.'

Kyam was looking down at his desk, picking his fountain pen up and placing it down again, and did not see Prendegast's expression.

'Mrs Scatcliffe's restaurant, sir,' said Kyam.

'What of it?'

'The reciprocal meal scheme.'

'Yes.'

'You will be aware of the complaints.'

'No.'

'There have been complaints.'

'About?'

'About the hygiene in the establishment. About the food. Too much of the meal is made from bananas. There have been complaints of food poisoning from the food. And about the proprietress herself, er, embarrassing the guests with her, er, singing.'

'Guests from this hotel have been visiting Mrs Scatcliffe's restaurant for twenty-five years.'

'We are not suggesting, sir, that they cease to do so, merely that the reciprocal meal basis is ended.'

'But Kyam – every single arsing hotel on this beach is now all-inclusive. No guest is going to fork out to eat locally when they're wasting the food and drink they've already paid for back in the hotel. That was part of the agreement at the takeover: if we went all-inclusive, the trips to Mrs Scatcliffe's would become part of the meal arrangement. Besides, she's Hyacinth's aunt.'

Kyam got to his feet, smiling understandingly, and moved round to sit on the front of his desk. If he had been a detective, at this moment he would have offered Prendegast a cigarette. He sensed the need to do something. 'Tic Tac?' he said, producing a carton of sweets from his trouser pocket.

'Fuck off.'

'For the modern visitor,' said Kyam, 'where once the Caribbean region represented an escape to barefoot freedom and relaxation, today's vacationer is looking to find standards of hygiene and accommodation not just equivalent to, but higher than, those he finds at home. The Caribbean holiday is perceived as aspirational; the holiday of a lifetime. The visitor is in search, not of authenticity but of a new Caribbean reality based on his experience of the region as reflected through advertising and vacation promotions. When this hotel began, the visitor was looking for very different things, sir.'

Prendegast was very still, except for one hand which was vibrating methodically on the desk.

'The visitor expresses the desire to experience local culture but it has been found that the most successful manner of presenting this is for the native to stage his own image within the tourist space.'

There was a full minute's silence.

'They can put the fish in my freezer in the cottage,' said Prendegast. 'The meal thing with Mrs Scatcliffe's had better continue' – suddenly he lunged at Kyam so that the small man jumped off the desk; Prendegast took hold of his ear – 'or else I shall have to tweak you.'

Darkness came quickly to St Theodore. At five-thirty the last histrionics of the sun – tearing and flinging cloud, plummeting downwards, flooding the sky with red, flaming the surface of the sea – were making the tourists on Grand Anse beach seriously rethink their lives. By six o'clock a hot, liquid blackness had engulfed the island and the amphitheatre of hills around the harbour of Georgetown were twinkling with light. Down in the port, floodlight blasted onto the massive white hulk of the Geest boat, three white cranes on deck standing ready for the morning.

Inside Mrs Scatcliffe's restaurant, the steamy darkness of
the jungle was pressing in on every side as if it were about to
leap over the verandah, strangling the chairs and tables with
creepers and heavy, rubbery leaves. There was the sound of
a vehicle labouring its way through the gears as it struggled
up the hill: the Spice Island bus come to collect the tourists. Right on cue, Mrs Scatcliffe's thin reedy voice rang out,
beginning her final hymn of praise just a little higher than
she could manage. Inside the thatched restaurant the dozen
or so tourists watched in various degrees of alarm as Mrs
Scatcliffe's arms began to rise in parallel, so that by the time
she reached the chorus and climax – 'Praise Him. Praise
Him. Praise be to Our Lord. Praise Him, Praise Him, Praise
be to Our Lord!' – they were held high on either side of her
head, where they remained for some time after the hymn
had finished.

The tourists were uncertain what to do now. There was
silence, apart from the high, regular beep of the frogs. A girl
tried applause and then tailed off. An American man, grey-
haired, in slacks and a yellow short-sleeved shirt, fumbled in
his pockets for change. Another American couple continued
to eat their food, looking miserable, flicking away flies.

'Praise be to Our Lord,' announced Mrs Scatcliffe eventually, before letting her arms fall, smiling knowingly and
making her way back into the kitchen.

'Well, I sure am glad I didn't eat any of that,' said the woman from the elderly American couple, pushing away a dark earthenware pot. 'I should be ill.'

'But it tasted good, Sharee,' said her husband.

'This is the real Caribbean,' said the young girl, eyes shining with an almost mystical conviction. 'This is the Caribbean the tourists never see. Look at this table. Spotless.'

As the Spice Island bus pulled up below, Mrs Scatcliffe emerged beaming from the kitchen to see her guests off and give them the Lord's blessing. As soon as they were gone, she closed up the restaurant and made her way down the stony path to the yard. The moon was drifting behind a ragged mess of cloud, casting a pale light on the contours of the hills and the dry stalks of the banana crop.

In the morning, as the first sunlight crept across the yard and the cock crowed, Hyacinth was up lighting the fire. Hearing her, the little ones began to emerge from the two huts, dressed in over-stretched Babygros and worn pyjamas. Sandra and Bernice started lecturing their kids before they were even out of their hut, fixing their hair, looking for lost items of clothing. Thomas was feeding the baby porridge, and trying to do up his trainers. Mrs Scatcliffe knocked at the side of Leonard's hut with her stick.

'Leonard!' There was no response.

'Leonard! It is the cutting day! And you got two pools your own vomit to clear in this yard!'

Mrs Scatcliffe took her stick, made her way up the two rough concrete steps of the pink hut and swung open the door. 'Eh?' she said, softly. 'You mash you face?'

'I'm alright.'

'What you mean, you is alright? Mash the size of mango on you face. You been fighting, boy?' Silence. 'You want I wash you face?'

'No.'

'Eh? It be cutting day for the banana and you sleeping in you bed?'

Outside, the others were watching the hut, straining their ears. There was a sudden bellow from Leonard. Then the door opened and Mrs Scatcliffe appeared. 'What you's all lookin at?' she said, and made her way down the concrete stairs. 'Bernice. You go fetch me iodine.'

Inside Leonard lay in the sweltering shack, holding his face, feeling the sweat prickling on his body. He reached under the bed and pulled up a half-empty bottle of dark rum.

By late afternoon the cranes on the Geest boat were working constantly, the road to the dock a line of trucks waiting to unload their fruit, the roads on the hillsides lined with families carrying their boxes of fruit to the graders, the Scatcliffe family amongst them.

'Leonard he do eat us out of house and home and then come the cutting day ...' muttered Bernice.

'Bernice, I will hear no more of this talk.' said Mrs Scatcliffe from behind. 'Leonard is flesh and blood with this family and every child have his good and his bad time.'

'How much you think we make today?'

Mrs Scatcliffe sucked on her lips. With the income from the restaurant and Hyacinth's wage, they just about kept the family of eleven afloat.

'When Delores send the boy from England, she say she sending money, then this Leonard say he have none ...'

'Bernice, it is no way way to begin with a boy to call him a lying man.'

They turned the brow of the last hill and looked down on the depot: a wooden warehouse, lit by hurricane lamps in a hollow by the roadside, thronging with people and vehicles. A lorry was reversing out, belching black exhaust fumes, scattering the crowd. The Scatcliffe party made their way down, through the gates into the crowd. A man, naked to the waist, strode past them with a pile of boxes on his head, glistening with sweat.

'Now, see, if we had Leonard here ...'

'Bernice,' said Mrs Scatcliffe. 'A woman do not clean out the skillet in the marketplace.'

Inside the shed a maze-like pathway made its way through the boxes stacked high. A rusty grill stretched from ceiling to floor and before it a line of dark, grease-soaked tables, a girl seated behind each on a tall stool, a chart, a measure and a set of weighing scales before her. There was hubbub and chatter, and the roar of engines.

Two hours later they were still waiting in the queue. Doreen and Bernice were off flirting. Thomas was minding the children and Mrs Scatcliffe stood with the bananas and maintained a high-lifted chin. Between them, Mrs Scatcliffe reflected, Hyacinth's wage from the Spice Island and the earnings from the restaurant could barely keep the family. She squatted and dozed a little, then a conversation on the other side of the row of boxes made her sit up.

'Nobody beat Leonard for drinking and lying. I aksed him, "What for you make a mockery of this family?" He told we he take shovel to we window. This Leonard is a scorpion.'

'I heard murderer.'

Mrs Scatcliffe poked her head between the boxes. The woman speaking was wearing a plastic shower cap.

'You go wash she mouth, Jean Kelly. Well might I aks myself how woman who married he scorpion herself feel move to pronounce.'

'How the banana, Mrs Scatcliffe?'

'Not so good, man, you know.'

The walls of the depot were covered with posters from Geest telling them to be careful about bruising when they packed, and showing a housewife in a supermarket in Britain putting back a hand of bananas with brown marks. 'I like my fruit clean,' she was saying.

Mrs Scatcliffe closed her eyes and prayed they would be lucky with the grader.

It was nine o'clock at night before their turn came. When they got near she shouted along the line for Thomas to come. It always worked best if there was a young man to flirt with the girl, but Thomas was only twelve, and when he was tired he looked like a boy, not a man, with his big eyes and diffident stance.

The girl was tired. She asked first for the two C-grade boxes. Opened them and looked, bored, at the fruit.

'D-grade,' she said.

'Eh?' began Mrs Scatcliffe.

'We don't take no more this mark here.'

She clicked her fingers at the pile for the next grade. Thomas pretended to misunderstand and pulled out one of the good boxes.

'Uh-uh,' she shook her head and clicked her fingers again.

Thomas brought out the box she wanted and laid it before her. She opened it, looked at three of the hands.

'No good,' she said, closing the box and writing a chit. 'That fourteen dollar for the two D-grade. The other you take away.'

'But the fruit is good. I got mouth to feed,' began Mrs Scatcliffe.

'You try in the market,' said the girl.

Hyacinth swung through the rubber doors into the kitchen carrying two plates – one of them containing three small portions of the crème caramel, the pineapple cherry rum flan and the lemon mousse, with a tiny spoonful taken out of each, and the other an untouched piece of Black Forest gateau. She went to her corner of the kitchen, wrapped them in paper and put them in her shopping bag. Then she returned to the Spice Island dining room. There was a table of four to clear, all buffets: two chicken breasts, a sweet-and-sour prawn, and one plate with three slices of ham, a portion of prawn cocktail, a piece of cheese and a spoonful of fish curry combined with a rice salad. Back to the kitchen she went, heading for her shopping bag.

'Excuse me. What are you doing there?'

She looked up. It was the short, clean figure of Kyam.

'Ah teaching myself to scuba dive, sir.'

Kyam looked momentarily nonplussed. He was, to the enormous pleasure of the staff, unable to differentiate between the rich imagery of the St Theodoran dialect, which he was supposed to appreciate and encourage, and people taking the piss.

'We cannot permit the taking of food. Any taking of food whatsoever is in theory, at least, considered by the company to be theft.'

Hyacinth stared at him uncomprehendingly for a moment and looked back at the food.

'You will understand, er ...' he peered at her badge.

'Doreen,' said Hyacinth.

Kyam peered again at the badge.

'Well, er, yes – if we do not enforce this particular rule there is no way of ensuring that wastage quotas are kept to an absolute minimum and your wages are kept high. Unless our staff clearly understand that they are not permitted to remove food from the premises or to consume any food other than in their own canteen, we have no way of ensuring that all the food intended for guests goes to the guests.'

'So what we do with the food that the guests don't eat?'

'You throw it away.'

Hyacinth stared at him. Then, without taking her gaze away from him, she lifted the lid of the rubbish bin and emptied the plates into it. Then she picked up her shopping bag. Took out the wrapped packages of dessert, unwrapped them and dropped them one by one into the bin.

'Such chupidness,' she said. 'It do make we vex.'

Leonard paused just below the steps to the restaurant, pulled on his joint and chucked it into the trees. He sloped up the stairs. It was six o'clock. Bit late. The bus was due in an hour. Upstairs the restaurant was in darkness. Normally the candles would be lit on the tables, and hanging in coconut shells from the roof. It was still, silent. There was a light in the kitchen. As he pushed open the door he saw Mrs Scatcliffe's slipper on the floor. She was slumped on the table, her head on her skinny wrinkled arms.

'Grandma,' he said, kneeling beside her. Her hand reached out and found his.

'Leonard, the Spice Island they do come no more to the restaurant.'

2

'JUST GOING FOR A STROLL, DARLING.' Geoff rose to his feet, made a palaver of folding his minuscule fax of the *New York Times* as if it were a full edition of the *Sunday Telegraph*, tucked it under his arm, picked up the room key, looked at Margaret, put the key back on the table, then set off towards the beach.

It had occurred to him one day that the point at which they had begun to call each other 'darling' was the point at which it had become irrevocably bad between them. On her part the 'darling' was placatory, a cajoling preface to avoid his irritation. For him it was ironic. It was a subtle way of giving vent to his disappointment with an ageing wife.

Margaret wrapped a couple of pieces of banana bread in a napkin for later and slipped it into her beachbag. She glanced across at the young couple breakfasting in the same pagoda. This was one of the charming features of the Spice Island: meals were taken under thatched canopies, dotted amongst the jungle foliage with two or three tables under each one. The girl was in a bait about something, sighing and tossing her long shiny black hair about. The man she was with looked intelligent, or was that just his spectacles? No. She could see his eyes now as he looked up from his book. He was clever. He looked amused, and tolerant. Late thirties, forty maybe. The girl rose to her feet, lithe and perfect in a simple black swimsuit. 'Of course, all the rooms had a sea view at K Club. They were all on the beach,' she said desolately. Then she turned and walked out of the restaurant, leaving her fruit plate untouched.

'Natasha,' said the man softly and held up the room key with its cumbersome wooden tag. My goodness, he was divine. Margaret looked down at her swimsuit with some regret. It had seemed a clever idea at the time, with a full top, almost like a blouse, taken in loosely at the 'waist' in order to make her stomach look like a balancing design feature. She wrapped her sarong round the offending thing.

The girl was tutting and tossing again now, grabbing the key and strutting off. Why was she wasting time being in a mood when she could have been taking him back with her while she was still so ... so young? She could be having sex with that lovely young man, while she still had slim, firm thighs and a flat stomach, instead of sulking and tutting. Would that Margaret herself had been born a couple of decades later. She could have stepped in now and comforted that poor young man. She started to giggle quietly to herself. Oh, it was nice being on holiday.

Later she was lying by the swimming pool beside Geoff. Geoff was beginning the process of going for a swim.

Margaret secretly very much enjoyed watching Geoff on holiday because stripped of his suit and and his office he had a bit of a struggle to keep his dignity. He stood up now and pulled up the waistband of his trunks as if they were his suit trousers, then coughed manfully and walked towards the pool with his mouth braced in an upside-down smile to separate him from the proceedings. At the edge of the pool he rubbed his hands together, and then jumped in. When he jumped, his expression suggested that it wasn't him jumping at all, it was someone else. Because, somehow, jumping in a swimming pool wasn't the sort of thing the Chairman of Northern Power did.

It was good to get him away from his work obsession and have some time just to themselves. And Margaret smiled as she watched him swimming with ... well, with tenderness.

There was the sound of a bell, and one of the room boys appeared, wearing a flowery shirt, ringing a handbell and holding up a sign with a name written on it in chalk. Margaret looked at the curly script. *Mr Enderbury*.

'It's you, love,' she called, pointing at it.

'Ah, right,' said Geoff, making his way to the steps. As he climbed up the ladder the weight of water in his trunks pulled them down so that half of his bottom stuck out at the top. He pulled them up brusquely as he strode over to where Margaret was and picked up his shirt and his towel.

'Will it be the office?' said Margaret, immediately thinking, *stupid question*.

'I expect so.' He wrapped the towel round his waist, put the shirt on and strode off – looking, she thought, like a child trying to be grown up in that outfit.

Margaret was reading the recipes in the February *Good Housekeeping*. There was nothing nicer, she thought, than lying by a pool feeling the sun on your skin – knowing you could plop into the pool any second but not doing – and reading a magazine. She felt the sweat trickling between her breasts. It was very hot, approaching noon. She moved the chair back a bit to be further under the umbrella and lay looking at the water in the pool – with the sunlight making patterns on the blue water like the string in a string bag, she thought. Then thought she was daft for thinking of string bags in the tropics.

And Hyacinth, who had just been in the office, listening while Geoff was taking his phone call, saw Margaret smiling at the pool as she passed on her way to the restaurant. 'Does the knife plunge into the pumpkin?' Hyacinth said softly to herself. 'Or does the pumpkin fall onto the knife?'

Margaret dozed off for a while, then opened her eyes. Geoff seemed to be taking a long time. She didn't have a watch with her. Maybe he was sorting out some problem. She suddenly caught a smell of baking wafting over from the kitchen. Like fresh bread with cinnamon or nutmeg. Maybe they'd go to the market in Georgetown one day and she could get some real nutmeg and vanilla pods. They were .75p in Sainsbury's, vanilla pods. Maybe she'd go back to the room and put a dress on for lunch, then go and rescue Geoff. The office ought to leave him alone when he was on holiday.

She gathered up her things, wondering whether it would be alright to leave the towels on the chairs over lunch. She made her way up the little pathway to the room, thinking how all the details of the hotel compound – the crazy paving on the path, the low-level lamps with two rings round the stem and metal lampshades – became so quickly familiar. All there just to make things nice. She was looking forward to getting back to the room. The maid would have done it. It would be cool with all the air conditioning.

When she put the key in the door, she found it already unlocked, and jumped. There was a smell of cigarette smoke and someone in the room.

Geoff was sitting in semi-darkness with the curtains closed, smoking, still wearing the shirt and the towel wrapped round his waist. Margaret stood just inside the door.

'Geoff?'

'Just leave me, Margaret. Please? Alright?'

'What is it?'

He said nothing.

'Is it the children?'

'I said, leave me.'

There was not a mood of his which she did not know, had not tried to soothe, taken on, tiptoed round, looked at every which way. When he was in this particular one, everything she would say would hang like a big, wrong fish. So over the years she had learned what to do now. Say nothing. Simply remove herself. But he looked so terrible.

'Geoff, what is it, love?'

'I said, leave me.' He looked down, lowered his voice. 'Please.'

She closed the door of the villa and stood in the enclosed garden, looking at the fountain playing onto the plunge pool, not knowing quite what to do. The view from the terrace was like a postcard: sand, crystal sea, yacht, small tropical island, absolutely cloudless blue sky. She looked at the double hammock and felt ridiculous. Everything seemed completely nonsensical, suddenly. It was supposed to be a romantic paradise.

Maybe she would go to lunch. She hesitated, let herself out of the gate at the back of the villa, then realised she had meant to put a dress on. The brochure said casual elegance. Did a swimsuit and turquoise towel qualify as casual elegance? She would tell them, if they mentioned it, that there had been an emergency. She set off carefully down the steep path. It was quite tricky to negotiate, but to be fair it had said 'Unsuitable for the elderly or infirm' in the brochure.

Maybe Geoff was involved in some dreadful disgrace like the Guinness affair which would call upon all her reserves of loyalty and affection. She would stand by him. She wouldn't go to pieces or have a nervous breakdown or anything. After all, they had been perfectly happy when they had no money and he was just in an ordinary job. More happy, in actual fact, than they were now. Anyway, she thought, don't be melodramatic. It was probably just share prices or something.

In the Pagoda she sat with her back to the sea, with an untouched prawn cocktail in front of her. There were two other couples having lunch.

'I've brought my golf clubs,' one of the husbands was saying to the other.

'Really? Going to play?'

'Yup.'

'Have you played in the West Indies before? Indonesia? Asia?'

Margaret wondered what they thought about her dining alone. Well, lots of couples must have lunch separately sometimes. There was a fly buzzing round her prawn cock-tail. She brushed it away and took a sip of water.

'I followed him round at the Open last year,' the American man was saying. 'Every time he swung the club, he swung it in exactly the same way.'

'Really? Exactly the same?'

She had to go back to Geoff. She saw the waitress watch-ing her – a big black woman, her broad round hips bulging in a straight, bright blue skirt. Margaret got to her feet and picked up her room key. The waitress approached her.

'Everything alright, ma'am?'

Margaret jumped. Did she know? Hyacinth looked straight into her eyes for a second – terrified. Like a rabbit.

'The food, ma'am?' she said, quietly.

'Oh yes, yes, lovely, thank you. Um. Too much, um, breakfast.'

When she returned to the room, Geoff was lying curled up on the bed, looking weak and ungainly. He was wearing a short-sleeved shirt made out of T-shirt material, with wider stripes at the bottom than at the top, and white synthetic tennis shorts.

'Margaret,' he said, still lying curled, not looking at her. 'I have been very foolish.'

'Foolish' was a schoolteacher's word. The sort of word you used when you were telling other people off. Not about yourself.

She sat down on the edge of the bed thinking that, whatever it was, she would comfort him, make it alright for him, and stand by him, because she loved him.

'Tell me.'

Geoff lay in agony, hating the Margaret caring voice and the guilt which it produced these days. Part of him wanted her to put her arms around him like Mummy and wipe the hurt away, and part of him wanted her to look like Jennifer. He sat up slowly and put his glasses on. On the bedside table, next to the hotel notepad and biro and stand-up card, there was a fax of the centre pages of a tabloid newspaper.

'You'd better look at this,' he said, in a professional tone, clearing his throat and handing it to her.

Aterwards she thought that, even in the most outrageous situations, there are ways of doing things, putting things, which are less hurtful and cause less harm than others. It just isn't true, she thought, that if a thing is going to hurt another person it will hurt them equally however you deal with it, so there is no need to think or try.

It was about as hurtful as could be to sit on the king-sized bed, with its colourful fabrics counterpoising the natural stone and wooden walls, looking beyond the outdoor shower, surrounded by bamboo and open to the elements, towards the crystal-clear waters and talcum powder sands, and to read in the *News of the World* what her husband had said to this woman who, unlike Margaret, was still young and beautiful, and to read what he had done with this woman in bed.

Sometimes she would return to that moment and stare at it in fascination as you might lift a dressing off a wound and stare at the unaccustomed break in your own skin. There was a patchiness of vision and a sensation in the centre of her, above the stomach, which made perfect sense of the expression 'broken heart'. With the self-blaming instinct of a woman, she instantly attributed his infidelity to her own inadequacy and felt ashamed. And in a flash of clarity she saw a pain-filled future stretching ahead and understood that nothing was going to be the same again and nothing was going to be as she had thought. And then her instinct was to turn to Geoff for comfort, because she always had, and because, in that place, he was all that she had. And for a few moments they lay on the king-sized bed and sobbed in each other's arms.

'Men and women are mortal enemies, angel. Mortal.'
'Course they bloody are, darling. Shall we have a mai tai?'

Hyacinth, on poolside duty now, watched as the two elderly English ladies teetered along the path from the pool area in their swimsuits. One was wearing a navy and white captain's hat, trimmed just above the peak with a gold rope bow. The other sported a fuchsia and lime-green patterned turban and was carrying a white quilted handbag with a gold chain strap. Both ladies were orange.

'Is there a shop here?'

'A what, angel?'

'Shop, darling. Shop, shop, shop.'

'Couldn't agree more, angel. Best thing to do. Bloody men.'

'Do you know? I'm completely exhausted.'

The women stopped in their tracks and looked at each other, wide-eyed at the sudden realisation.

'It's been a very tiring morning.'

'Very tiring.'

'My nerves are shot to ribbons.'

'Don't think about it.'

'I mean, it's a very long pool.'

'Olympic. It's an Olympic-sized pool.'

'Pool? It's the size of the bloody Red Sea.'

'Shall we sit down?'

'I think we should, you know. I really am feeling very tired.'

They pushed the paperbacks and suntan lotion off the nearest pair of sunloungers and then flopped onto the beds.

'I'm not going to leave you, of course,' was the first thing Geoff had said. 'We'll go back to England together, Margaret, side by side, and face the music and tell them that you're standing by me.'

Margaret got to her feet and made her way unsteadily into the bathroom. Suddenly she thought her heart was going to break, because on one side of the washbasin was her Oil of Ulay bottle and flowery toilet bag and, on the other side, his Imperial Leather shaving foam bottle, his black, grey and red manly toilet bag, placed as these items had been placed in various homes and hotel rooms for a quarter of a century.

She washed her eyes and applied powder and lipstick. Geoff watched her from the bed, thinking, without actually knowing he was thinking this, doesn't she realise that with her hair like that, short and grey, she looks like an old lady, not the sort of woman who should be with me? And Margaret looked up in the mirror, and read the end of this expression in his eyes and she knew that at least in the immediate future – and she was thinking about seconds and minutes rather than anything longer term – she wanted to get away.

'Do you think we could get one of those divine boys to bring us a mai tai?'

'Oh, angel, I don't know,' wailed the lady in the captain's hat, suddenly overwrought. 'I don't know if they will.' Hyacinth, listening from behind the foliage, started to smile.

'I'm very thirsty,' gasped the other.

'Can I help you ladies?' said Hyacinth, approaching. The two women looked up at her with huge saucer eyes.

'Oh, darling, would you?' whispered the lady in the captain's hat, weak with gratitude. She wore lipstick the colour of mango arranged in a generous oval around her lips. 'You see, we're terribly thirsty ...'

'... and we wanted a mai tai.'

They gazed up at her guiltily, as if they'd asked for a toy boy.

'I'll see to that for you.'

'Darling! Don't carry it yourself,' said the one in the captain's hat. 'They're very heavy. Oh my God, look – there's that poor lovely woman who's married to that silly bloody man.'

They all looked up at the hillside, where Margaret was making her way distractedly down the path again, still in her swimsuit.

'Bloody man.'

The lady in the peaked hat beckoned Hyacinth down. 'Silly bloody fool. Up and down the bloody beach all day raising his absurd hat at air hostesses. Old enough to be their great-uncle.'

'Great-great-uncle more like, darling.'

'Silly bloody fool. Treats her like a retard.'

Hyacinth looked quickly behind her. 'Some man is scorpion,' she said in a low voice. 'He carry a sting.'

'Darling, you're absolutely right.'

'Completely right.'

'Snakes. Scorpions.'

'Vipers.'

'Beasts from the bowels of the earth.'

'I'll send a boy to bring you you's drinks,' said Hyacinth, backing off.

'Oh darling, you are lovely,' growled the fuchsia-turban lady, wrinkling her nose.

'One of the nice tall ones.'

'Thank you, angel,' said the other, putting her hand weakly on her heart.

'No problem,' said Hyacinth. 'Don't you stay out here

too long, now. There's a hole up there.'

'You know she's absolutely right,' they were saying as she walked away. 'It is very hot.'

'Well, it's like a furnace.'

'Darling. It is a furnace. The sun is a furnace.'

'I mean, if you looked straight at it, it would burn your eyeballs out in a second.'

'You'd be dead in a trice. You wouldn't know a thing about it.'

'Dead as a post, darling.'

'Stone dead. Did I tell you I joined a health club?'

'How much?'

'Angel, I'm going to have to say it quickly. Five thousand pounds.'

'Oh darling, look at the poor woman. We're going to have to get her a drink.'

'Darling!' they called weakly. 'Darling!', finally getting Margaret's attention. 'Come over here and have a mai tai.'

Afterword

IT WAS EINSTEIN WHO FIRST QUESTIONED whether 'ether' existed in the air. Up until then, scientists hadn't doubted it. Light travelled through an invisible form of matter, and that matter was called ether. Not so, said Einstein. Light simply travelled where no matter existed. As tended to be the case, Einstein was right. And just like that, the air around us changed.

Around the world today, something similar is happening. The air is becoming unfamiliar once again. The changing climate is bringing with it strange, disarming stories. Stories of people's lives forced in new, unwanted directions. Stories of confusing and unpredictable weather. Stories with endings no-one knows. At Oxfam, we're responding to more and more of them.

Under postcard-blue skies in Sakhira, Bangladesh, people tell stories of 'tiger widows'. Bengal tigers have always lived among the knotted mangrove trees of the Sundarbans forest. But in recent years, worsening floods have destroyed large areas of the forest, and the tigers have started roaming closer to bordering villages in search of food. At the same time, struggling farmers – their rice paddies ruined because salt water from rising seas has entered the soil – have started foraging deeper in the Sundarbans, also looking for food, as well as for timber. It's a lethal mix, fuelled by changing weather conditions, and one which has made 'tiger widow' a terrifying everyday phrase here.

Thousands of miles away, across the Pacific Ocean in Peru, people talk about the 'dying' glaciers of the Cordillera Blanca mountain range. The views in this strip of sparkling natural beauty remain as breathtaking as the altitude. But the landscape is changing dangerously. Glaciers are shrinking, melting much more quickly than they can replenish themselves. Villagers who live beneath the mountains are already seeing local rivers – which flow with glacial meltwater – get shallower in the dry season. If things continue as they are, many of the region's glaciers will disappear completely within the next fifteen years. In a country where people rely on the meltwater to drink, to irrigate their crops and to power hydroelectric plants, the consequences will be dire. And not just for those who live in the shadow of the mountains; everyone in Lima, the capital, depends on this water, too.

Climate change is the author of thousands of stories like these. Oxfam staff are hearing them all over the world. People are seeing changes. Right now. Today. Climate change is often still portrayed as a problem for the future. But millions of people already know that's not the case.

Weather that used to be reliable and predictable is now anything but. The basic patterns that have defined people's lives for generations are unravelling. Where the rainy season used to last for four months, it's now lasting for six. Or eight. Or not coming at all. Where rains used to arrive and nourish crops, they are coming in torrents and destroying them.

Where people used to walk for five minutes to collect water, they are walking for an hour or more because water sources have dried up. The effects of climate change are complex and still difficult to track – in some places, drought is the biggest danger; in others, heavier rains and increased flooding pose the greatest threat. But the planet is already getting warmer. The science is unequivocal. And the stories of people's lives getting much more difficult because of changing weather are everywhere.

And that, in a nutshell, is why Oxfam is involved, and why earlier this year we launched our *Here & Now* climate change campaign. This is a crisis with humanity at its heart. Climate change affects people. It costs lives. And the people most at risk are people living in poverty.

There are a host of reasons why this is the case. When you have a close relationship with natural resources, as many people in developing countries do, your life is turned upside down when crops don't grow or water stops flowing. The same is true if you live in an unplanned settlement in an area prone to the kinds of extreme weather events – floods, cyclones and so on – which climate change will make more frequent and intense. And when disaster does strike, few poor people have savings or insurance to fall back on. So losing everything means exactly that, and that makes the fight to escape poverty much more difficult.

It's an outrageous injustice. The people least responsible for climate change are being hit hardest by its effects. Or, to put it another way, the average Bangladeshi contributes 0.3 tonnes of carbon dioxide to the atmosphere every year. The average American contributes 20 tonnes. That's the kind of inequality that has prompted thousands of Oxfam campaigners to push for genuine and equitable political action. We know what's needed – at least an 80 per cent reduction in greenhouse gas emissions by 2050 – and we know the technology exists for this to be achieved. What's needed is political will. It's the responsibility of the rich, greenhouse-gas-guzzling nations to take a lead in taming the monster they've created. Time is running out. The world needs binding commitments to tackle climate change. Now.

As well as campaigning, Oxfam is working to help people adapt to changing weather, and to prepare for the effects of climate change that are already inevitable. In south-eastern Peru, whole communities are working to make sure everyone knows what to do and where to go during a flood. In Eritrea and Zimbabwe, farmers are growing drought-resistant crops. In Cambodia, people are using new, more efficient techniques to grow rice, ensuring they get as much as possible from their land. And in Bangladesh, people are raising the foundations of their homes above rising flood levels, as well as building flood shelters and storing more food and fuel in high places, safe from floodwaters. These are just a few of the projects we're involved in. Because ignoring what's happening isn't an option.

The air around us is changing. We have no choice but to confront our new reality. It's still possible to write stories about climate change that end with justice being done. But there's no time to waste. Climate change costs lives. Let's sort it. *Here & Now.*

oxfam.org.uk/hereandnow

208